Also by these authors and available from New English Library:

THE HOOK

SAHARA STRIKE

Denis Cleary and
Frank Maher

NEW ENGLISH LIBRARY/TIMES MIRROR

The characters in this book are fictitious and any resemblance to actual persons, living or dead, is purely coincidental.

A New English Library Original Publication, 1980

First NEL Paperback Edition February 1980

NEL Books are published by
New English Library Limited from
Barnard's Inn, Holborn,
London EC1N 2JR.
Made and printed in Great Britain by
C. Nicholls & Company Ltd,
The Philips Park Press, Manchester

45004302 9

To our wives, Joan and Kate, with gratitude for their forbearance and help during the writing.

Get weapons, ho!
And raise some special officers of night.

Othello, Act I

CHAPTER ONE

Madame Mercier glanced up from her accounts book as the big man came down the stairs into the tiny foyer of the Pension Paul.

'Bonjour, m'sieur.'

He placed his room key in front of her. She picked it up and felt the usual little *frisson* of excitement as she looked into the slate-grey eyes regarding her from the other side of the reception desk. Two months had passed since this man with the – to her – almost unpronounceable name had taken a room at her *pension*. From that time the morning ritual had, in some strange way, become important to her. At her age, it was perhaps foolish to indulge in fantasies, but she knew that there was something about him that set him apart from all others and this attracted and intrigued her.

'Bonjour, madame.'

She watched as he walked to the open front door, and was reminded once again of the leopard in the Zoological Gardens. This man had all the grace of movement and fluid co-ordination of that big cat, but unlike it, he carried a sign that said 'Warning – Do not touch'. With a regretful sigh, Madame Mercier picked up her pen and returned to her accounts.

Breakenridge stood on the top step of the *pension* entrance, eyes quartering the busy street. Although it was only 9.30 in the morning, the Rue Lafayette was already baking in the hot July sun. Housewives lingered in the patches of shade cast by shop awnings, chattering, reluctant to move on. A never-ending stream of traffic flowed sluggishly towards the Gare St-Charles. To the untrained eye, everything appeared normal, just another day. But for Breakenridge, it was different. Today he was going to flush the bastards out of hiding. The hunters – whoever they were – were about to become the hunted. From this moment on, the game had changed. So had the rules.

Casually he took a battered pack of Disque Bleu from the inside pocket of his pale blue denim sports jacket and, extracting a cigarette, lit it with a silver Dunhill. He looked at the lighter for a moment, his mouth tightening in a mirthless smile as he remembered the woman who had given it to him. The first of the promised pieces of silver. The Judas gift.

Slipping it back into his pocket, he moved onto the pavement and sauntered towards the junction with Rue Jemmapes. At the corner he stopped at the news-stand and bought a *Herald Tribune.* He opened it, apparently studying the front page. From this vantage-point he was able to scan four streets. Nothing triggered off any signals as yet. But they were there. The hard-won awareness, refined again and again over the years, told him he was not mistaken.

Folding the paper, he continued unhurriedly along Rue Jemmapes, crossing Rue Villeneuve. At a pavement café he ordered coffee and croissants and sat at a table under the striped awning, his back to the wall, reading his paper.

In the fifteen minutes it took to finish his breakfast, he had noted two possibles. One, a fat man in a crumpled white suit, stood outside a *tabac* reading a newspaper. The other, a smartly dressed man, was gazing intently into the window of a car showroom on the opposite side of the street.

Breakenridge left the café, passing close to the fat man outside the *tabac.* Nothing registered. Reaching the next corner, he glanced back. Neither man had moved or looked in his direction.

Crossing the street, he entered Rue Canon and entered a tiny garage. Nodding to a mechanic bent over the entrails of an ancient Renault, he stepped into a battered white Peugeot 404, started up and reversed out into the street. There was no sign of either the fat man or the window-gazer. He shrugged. If they knew his routine, they'd be in a car.

Cutting through a maze of one-way streets, he kept close watch on his rear-view mirror.As he turned into Rue Roger he was sure. Three cars back hung the metallic green Citroen 2400 he'd noticed almost at the start. He grinned, slid the gear lever into third and put his foot down. The Peugeot surged forward, carving up an elderly Simca. Behind, the Citroen pulled out and took up the chase. A few minutes later, Breakenridge was on the Cannes Autoroute.

He wound the Peugeot up to the legal limit. The Citroen stayed with him. Just before the Municipal Stadium, Breakenridge turned right off the Autoroute, then made a left turn into Avenue Centrale. He pulled the car to a stop outside a café, switched off the engine and sat for a moment. There was no sign of the Citroen. He got out of the car, walked into the café and sat down at a table by the window. A few minutes later the Citroen appeared, coming from the opposite direction. It cruised slowly past the Peugeot, then swung into a parking slot outside a café across the street. The driver got out and went inside. It was the window-gazer from the car showroom in Rue Jemmapes.

Breakenridge ordered a coffee, placed his folded paper on the table, selected a toothpick from the container in front of him, placed it between his teeth then, with a leisurely air, left, crossed the street and walked to the Citroen.

Crouching down beside the nearside front wheel, he unscrewed the dustcap, took the toothpick from his mouth and jammed it in the valve. He waited some moments, watching the tyre deflate; then, with the same leisurely air, he went back to the café, sat down, opened his paper and began reading.

He sensed the other man's presence. Without looking up from his paper he said quietly, 'You have until I finish my coffee, mister.'

He placed the paper on the table. The other man looked down at Breakenridge for a moment, suddenly aware of the cold menace reaching out from the big American. He repressed a slight shiver and licked dry lips.

'It will take some time to explain. But not here and now.' The man's English was almost without accent.

Breakenridge lifted his coffee cup. 'Take what I'm offering, sonny. Believe me, it's all you've got!' He drank and put the cup back down on the table.

Breakenridge watched as the other pulled out a chair and sat. He placed him around thirty-five and in good shape. The clothes were quietly expensive, a Tissot watch showing at the edge of his left cuff. White scar-tissue marred the cheekbone beneath the right eye. The fair hair was cut short and well groomed. He judged him to be a man more used to giving orders than taking them. The next few minutes could be very interesting. The man leaned in close.

'My name is Guillard,' he said softly. 'I am working with French Security on a matter of considerable importance.' He paused, as if unsure of what to say next. Breakenridge sipped his coffee.

'Go on,' he said.

Guillard glanced towards the counter, then back at Breakenridge.

'I must obtain clearance before telling you any more. Will you wait while I telephone?'

Breakenridge shrugged. 'Whatever you have to do is fine by me.'

He lit a Disque Bleu as Guillard went to the counter and asked the proprietor for a *jeton* for the telephone.

Right now, so far as Breakenridge was concerned, nothing made any sense. For at least a week – and maybe longer – someone had been following him, checking on every move he made. Then, when he forced that someone out into the open, the guy claimed to be French Security. If true, what the hell was he to them? As far as he knew he'd done nothing to draw their attention, and anyway, if they'd wanted to pick him up they could have done so at any time in the last six months. So, if Guillard was on the level there had to be a pay-off. If not . . . Breakenridge stubbed out the cigarette.

Guillard returned to the table and sat down. He took an envelope from his inside jacket pocket and slid it across the table.

'For you.' He nodded to the envelope. 'A thousand American dollars.'

Breakenridge did not even spare a glance for the envelope. 'Why?'

A faint smile flickered and died on Guillard's face. 'For goodwill?'

'I don't have any.'

For an instant, Guillard looked perplexed. Then his face cleared. Obviously the American was making a joke.

'I'd prefer to continue our business in your car.'

Breakenridge reached out for the envelope, put it in his pocket and stood up.

'Pay for the coffee,' he said flatly, and headed for the door.

He walked to the Peugeot and got into the front passenger seat. Across the street the Citroen leaned forlornly on its front tyre. As Guillard approached the Peugeot, Breakenridge leaned across and opened the driver's door. Guillard slid behind the wheel and shut the door.

'You don't take any chances,' he said wryly. Breakenridge shifted to face him.

'Slide the seat forward and put your hands on the wheel.'

'There's no need to—'

Breakenridge cut across the protest. 'Do it,' he said coldly.

Guillard shrugged and complied. 'Anything else?' There was an edge of sarcasm in his voice.

'You talk. I'll listen.'

For a moment Guillard looked into the grey eyes fixed unwaveringly upon him, then turned to stare out of the windscreen.

'It was not intended that you and I should meet this soon or in this way. However, no harm has been done. It has now been agreed for me to go ahead and put a certain proposition to you. A proposition, Mr Breakenridge, which I know you will have great difficulty in refusing.'

He turned his head and looked at the American. There was a subtle air of confidence about him now that disturbed Breakenridge slightly.

'Go on,' he said curtly.

Guillard nodded. 'One thing you should know, we have a very complete dossier on you. I won't bore you with the minor details. However, there are certain points of interest in your record that have considerable bearing on your present position. Overlooking the events which led to your hasty departure from Angola, let us concern ourselves with your illegal entry into South-West Africa in January, 1976.'*

He paused as if expecting a reaction from the other. If so, he was disappointed. Not a flicker of interest or emotion showed on Breakenridge's face.

*See *The Capricorn Run*, NEL, 1978

'Item one: the deaths of four members of the South African Defence Forces. Item two: the killing of a storekeeper. Item three: the kidnapping of Elizabeth Potgieter, a South African national.' Guillard's voice was coldly dispassionate, as though itemising a grocery list.

'By the way,' he went on, 'it may interest you to know that in her statement to the police, she mentions quite strongly that in the circumstances you treated her as well as could be expected. I find that interesting.'

Again, Breakenridge's face showed nothing. Behind the mask, however, his mind was reliving the final moments of that bloody morning when so many died. He saw again the jeep roaring at him, the girl crouched behind the wheel, heard his voice shouting as he tried to warn her, to stop her, felt the earth coming up to meet him and the pain from his wounded arm. Remembered the receding sound of the engine, the silence, the loneliness.

'I'm glad she made it,' he said quietly.

Guillard savoured a small moment of triumph. It was possible to get a reaction from the American after all.

'Perhaps you would not be so glad if you knew that she had given a complete description of you.' He smiled. 'It's all in the warrant the South African police have issued for your arrest. I can show you a copy.' He waited.

For the first time, those grey eyes moved off him to stare blankly out at the sunlit Avenue Centrale where life seemed so apparently uncomplicated.

After a few moments Breakenridge said, 'I hear you loud and clear.'

'Good.' Guillard sounded almost cheerful. 'It saves the usual time-wasting routine of questions and answers. I'm so pleased that you were quick to appreciate your position. After all, there's no need for embarrassment. We both know where we stand.'

'Get to it,' said Breakenridge harshly.

Guillard took a hand off the wheel as if to move his seat back into a more comfortable position.

'Leave it!'

Guillard eyed Breakenridge for a moment, then sighed and placed his hand back on the wheel.

'Six months ago', he began, 'a French archaeological expedition were exploring in the area of Assa in Morocco. The team consisted of six men and two women under the leadership of Professor Albert Dumont, a man of world-wide reputation and respect in his particular field. One of the two women was his wife. A group of Polisario guerillas raided their camp, killed one of the team, took the rest hostage and made a successful escape across the border into Algeria.'

He paused, wiped a bead of sweat from his forehead, then went on. 'Certain unacceptable demands have since been made on the French Government through Algerian channels with the hostages as the bargaining factor. A deadline was set and passed. A few days later we received proof that their intentions were serious.'

He gestured to his suit jacket. 'I would like to show you something. May I?'

Breakenridge nodded. 'Go ahead.'

He watched as Guillard took a small manila envelope from his inside pocket and held it out to him. Breakenridge took it, opened the flap. Inside were four small photographs in colour. Each one, taken from a slightly different angle, showed the severed head of a man resting in a plain wickerwork basket.

Answering Breakenridge's unspoken question, Guillard said: 'Professor Dumont. The basket was found outside our Embassy gates in Algiers after an anonymous telephone call. Naturally, the Algerian Government denied any involvement. But through our agents we have established that the hostages are being held in an old Legion fort in southern Algeria, and that men of the Algerian army have been seen there, apparently assisting the guerillas.'

'And –?'

'Ten days ago a decision was reached in Paris to go in, release the hostages and bring them out. The Department were faced with two problems: how and who? We resolved the "how". And now we have the answer to the second problem. You!'

'The hell you do!' Breakenridge leaned forward, eyes gleaming with anger.

Guillard shook his head in mock surprise. 'Surely you haven't already forgotten the earlier part of our conversation?'

Breakenridge stayed glaring at him for a moment, then slowly sank back in his seat.

'Why me, fercrissake?'

'Because of your reputation. And because you are here. Also, we know that you are in touch with others of your "trade". It should be no problem for you to raise a team and do the job.'

'Suppose I do as you ask. What happens afterwards?'

Guillard shrugged. 'You could continue to live in France for as long as you wish with no fear of the South African authorities. We would not be ungrateful.'

Sixty long seconds ticked away on Guillard's Tissot as Breakenridge apparently considered his position. Then he sighed.

'All right! I admit you've got me between a rock and a hard place. But hear me: getting into a place like Algeria with the necessary men and equipment ain't exactly like a Saturday morning stroll down Main Street.'

Guillard smiled foxily. 'We have the means to get you in and bring the hostages out. No problem.'

Breakenridge raised an eyebrow. 'Convince me.' He was heavily sceptical.

'I'll do better than that,' said Guillard. 'I'll show you.'

CHAPTER TWO

The Avenue Roger Salengro sweltered in the heat as the traffic built up to the usual mid-day rush. Local traffic clogged the junction at the Place Cazemajou. Massive juggernauts ploughed through from the dock area, heading for the Autoroute to Avignon and Nimes. It was no place for a man in a hurry, and Guillard acted as though he had all the time in the world, driving the Peugeot with all the sedateness of a nun returning from confession. Beside him, Breakenridge took careful note of their route. This was a section of Marseilles unfamiliar to him and he would need every scrap of information if he had to make a run for it. He still did not trust this man Guillard and up to now there was no actual proof that he was who he said he was.

The Peugeot slowed as it came abreast of the gas and electricity power-station complex and turned right. The white-on-blue street sign read 'Rue Pierre Aumont'. Grimy deserted buildings closed in on either side. A couple of long-abandoned cars rusted on a small area of wasteland. The whole place was a sad monument to industrial failure. Breakenridge tensed, nerve ends tingling. If anything was going to happen, this was the perfect place for it.

Guillard eased the Peugeot to a stop in front of a pair of heavy wooden gates set in a high brick wall. Across the street, behind high wire fencing, were parked a number of big trucks and trailers. Apart from themselves, there was not another human being in sight.

'This is it,' he said.

Switching off the ignition, he removed the key and turned. Two inches from his right eye was the muzzle of a .32-calibre Beretta automatic. A slight frown creased his forehead.

'I detect an obvious lack of trust on your part.'

Breakenridge ignored the Gallic sarcasm. 'Up yours,' he said flatly and held out his other hand for the ignition key. Guillard surrendered it with an air of faint annoyance.

'You said you were going to show me something.'

Guillard nodded in the direction of the heavy wooden doors. 'In there.'

Outside the car, the heat was oppressive, trapped between the tall buildings. Guillard loosened his tie, walked ahead of Breakenridge to a wicket gate set in one of the wooden doors, took a key from his pocket, inserted it in a mortise lock and turned it. The door swung back on well-oiled hinges.

Beyond was a wide cobblestone yard, grass sprouting in the cracks. A high brick wall surrounded the yard. At the far end was an old two-storey warehouse with a massive steel-shuttered sliding door set in its centre. To Breakenridge it appeared about as welcoming as a graveyard on open day.

They started across the yard, Breakenridge four paces behind, the Beretta firmly centred on Guillard's spine. As they drew closer to the building, a small door opened and a man stepped out.

Breakenridge moved in fast behind Guillard, jamming the gun hard into his back. Guillard winced at the pain, and stood stock still.

To the other man he said: 'This is the American. As you can see, he is short on trust. I suggest you walk ahead of us into the warehouse.'

The man shrugged, turned and led the way inside. Breakenridge stood for a moment letting his eyes adjust to the musty dimness. They were in a small cramped hallway whose peeling walls added to the general air of decay permeating the building. A narrow staircase disappeared into the darkness of the upper storey. It was a perfect killing ground.

The Beretta jabbed viciously into Guillard's spine. It was more effective than a Telex. He winced again and nodded to the other man: 'Carry on.'

Beside the staircase was a door. The man pushed it open and walked through. A few paces inside, he stopped. Sounds drifted through into the hallway, metal against metal, the humming of machinery, voices, movement, all strangely muffled. All Breakenridge could see was a large expanse of empty floor beyond the open door. Nothing was making sense.

He prodded Guillard forward. Inside, the reason for the sounds being muffled became instantly obvious. One half of the enormous floor area was concealed behind a number of heavy tarpaulins suspended from the roof beams. Whatever activity was in progress lay on the other side of them.

'It must be obvious by now,' Guillard said wearily, 'that nobody intends harming you. If we had, you'd have been very dead at any time in the last five minutes.' He turned to face Breakenridge. 'Do you accept that?'

Breakenridge stared at him for a long moment, then lowered the hammer on the Beretta and put the gun in his jacket pocket.

'Let's just say,' he drawled, 'the choices are limited.'

There was a tinge of relief in Guillard's answering grin. Being around Breakenridge was rather like being taken on a tour of a firework factory by a pyromaniac.

'Then let me show you the reason for your journey.'

He led the way to where the tarpaulin met the rear wall and pulled it aside. Breakenridge stepped through, took a few paces forward, then stopped. If he'd been expecting something spectacular, then the sight that met his eyes was a distinct let-down.

In the centre of the floor stood a truck. Or, to be technically exact, a thirty-six-ton Mercedes heavy-duty two-axle semitrailer tractor. Not that Breakenridge was aware of these technicalities. In fact he would have cared less had he been told. Disbelief and bewilderment were his over-riding emotions at this point in time.

'Our Trojan Horse,' Guillard announced with a touch of pride.

'You,' said Breakenridge heavily, 'have got to be putting me on.'

He stared at the scene in front of him. Against the far wall was a long work-bench. A man in overalls stood at a humming lathe, strips of metal spiralling to the floor. Tools of every description were scattered everywhere. Showers of sparks fountained around a figure in protective gear as he cut into aluminium sectioning with oxy-acetylene equipment. Other overalled men worked at varied tasks on and around the giant vehicle and its two trailers. Whatever they had in mind, the activity conveyed an air of speed and efficiency.

Guillard moved over to stand beside the forward-tilted cab and launched into what sounded suspiciously like a sales pitch.

'There are two bunks fitted with safety nets and retaining belts behind the driver, each with a separate light. Adjustable warm and cold air blower.'

His voice became noticeably enthusiastic as he warmed to his subject. Pointing to the top of the cab, he went on: 'A roof flap for additional ventilation. So you will at least be comfortable on your journey. A good product, the Mercedes,' he added. 'Naturally, had time permitted, we would have supplied a French vehicle.'

'Mister, I don't give an ounce of powdered shit who made the goddamn thing, I ain't here to buy it!'

Guillard glanced at him reproachfully, then gestured to the rear of the cab where a mechanic was working on the exposed V10 diesel engine.

'A three hundred and twenty brake horse power,' he began. At that moment, the mechanic pressed the starter button and the huge engine roared into life. As Guillard's lips continued to move soundlessly, the mechanic winked at Breakenridge.

Guillard gave up the hopeless contest and, beckoning to Breakenridge, made for the two trailers. The rear doors of the main trailer were open and Breakenridge could see that considerable alterations had already been made to the interior.

At the front end of the trailer, occupying its full width, had been built what appeared to be a storage compartment some six feet in depth and about three feet high. Attached to the front of this compartment, again occupying the full width of the trailer, was a black, ribbed metal tank with two filler caps, one at either end. Narrow fold-up bunks, four in number, had been rigged on both sides, ahead of the central doors of the trailer. To the rear of these doors, and extending back to within about four feet of the rear doors, was vertical metal racking with spring clips designed obviously to hold arms and equipment.

Breakenridge lit a Disque Bleu and thoughtfully studied the whole set-up. Slowly the possibilities began to emerge. Maybe, just maybe, it could work. After all, it had worked once before.

He grinned. A Trojan Horse. But this time three hundred and twenty of 'em. Diesel powered!

'You got someplace we can talk?'

The question was blunt. Guillard looked at him in surprise.

'Well, yes, but you haven't seen the rest.'

'I don't need to. Not right now.'

Guillard shrugged and led the way to a small glass-fronted office on the other side of the warehouse.

'You got a plan,' said Breakenridge. 'Let's hear it.'

He perched on the corner of an old and battered roll-top desk, listening intently as the other man outlined the basics of the operation.

'As soon as possible you recruit your team. The numbers and composition of this we leave to your judgement, naturally. Unfortunately, because of the time element and other considerations – mainly security – you will not be able to assemble them here for a briefing before you go.'

'Which is when?'

'Four days from now.'

'Four days?' Breakenridge echoed. 'Not possible!'

'I'm afraid it has to be,' Guillard said quietly. 'A new deadline has been set. Ten days from now they start killing the hostages. One every twenty-four hours. Unless of course the French Government agrees to their demands. Which it will not do.'

'Hold it.' Breakenridge came to his feet. 'If I can't get my team together and brief 'em before we go, then how in hell am I supposed to work this operation?'

Guillard appeared not in the least disturbed by Breakenridge's question.

'We have a "safe house" in Oran. Your men will assemble there and a pick-up point will be laid on. *Then* you can have your briefing. It's all being arranged.'

Breakenridge felt the net being drawn tighter around him. These French bastards were screwing him into the woodwork.

'It had better work,' he growled.

'It will.'

Guillard was confidence itself. He walked to the desk, opened a drawer and took out a large brown folder and a map. It was the Michelin 153, Africa North and West. He spread it out on the desk-top.

'Oran.' His finger tapped the map. 'Arrival there by ferry four days from now. Pick up your men here.' His finger slid over the map, moving south. 'This is the Trans-Saharan Motor Route, the N6. Through Bechar to Adrar and Reggane. A good road. But, from hereon, a bad surface. Vehicles can only travel in convoy.'

Breakenridge frowned. 'How do we solve that one?'

'No problem,' Guillard said airily. 'You simply fall back and disappear at the right moment.'

'Of course.' Breakenridge's face was innocent of expression. 'I'm glad I thought of that.'

He got a sideways glance from Guillard.

'Some very difficult stretches.' The finger resumed its march south. 'Here,' the finger stabbed at a point on the map, 'four hundred and seventy-five of your miles, is the fort. It was abandoned by the Legion years ago.'

'What's the enemy strength?'

'Approximately twelve guerillas are there permanently. And anything varying from half a company down to a platoon of Algerian regular troops, always under the command of an officer.'

'Can't you be more accurate?'

'It's the best we can do.'

'Uhuh. Now tell me about the way out.'

'Destroy the second trailer, alter the external appearance of the cab and main trailer, change the number plates. Then drive back up the road, through Adrar, to this point. Sbaa. Here there is a track heading west to the Moroccan border. A reception party will be waiting to bring you all back to France. Oh, just one thing. Leave no one alive at the fort. You understand?'

'Wasn't intending to,' Breakenridge assured him dryly.

Guillard picked up the brown folder and tipped a sheaf of photographs onto the map.

'These are air and satellite pictures for you to study.'

As Breakenridge spread them out, Guillard took a bottle and two plastic cups from another drawer. 'Cognac?'

Breakenridge nodded. Something on one of the satellite pictures caught his eye.

'What's that?' he asked casually.

Guillard leaned over his shoulder and studied the picture.

'An oil rig,' he said after a moment, 'I think.'

'Don't think,' said Breakenridge sharply. 'Be sure.'

Guillard leaned closer. 'An oil-rig. Definitely.'

'And that?' Breakenridge pointed.

'An airstrip. Probably a relic of the war in Algeria with the FLN.'

Breakenridge sipped his cognac and lit a cigarette, studying the map and the satellite pictures. His fingers rolled the silver lighter round and round in his big hand.

'Your plan,' he said finally.

Guillard waited expectantly.

'The way in. That can be made to work. The way out,' he shook his head slowly. 'Forget it!'

'Why?'

'Too many things can go wrong after we hit that fort. That's when it's gonna be rough. We're taking the long way in. The way out has got to be different. Unexpected. And,' he paused as if to give his words more weight, 'we need a back-up.'

'A back-up?' Guillard sounded puzzled. 'What sort of back-up?'

'I'll let you know,' Breakenridge said quietly.

CHAPTER THREE

Breakenridge stood near the Air Inter arrival gate at Marseilles/Marignane airport. The last incoming flight from Paris had touched down five minutes ago. He checked his watch. 21.20. The passengers should be coming through anytime now. It was almost twelve hours since he'd left his room in the Rue Lafayette, and it had been one hell of a day. The long session with Guillard in the warehouse, poring over maps and photographs, checking and double-checking on every single part of the operation, making innumerable lists of arms and equipment, going over and over the truck and trailers until he knew practically every inch of them, had left him drained. What he really needed right now was a shower, a drink and a porterhouse steak, in that order. But that would have to wait. The only consoling thought he had was that Guillard was, if anything, more tired.

The first trickle of passengers from the Paris plane straggled through the arrivals gate. He glanced across the busy concourse. Guillard's two watchdogs were still in evidence by the news stand, making no attempt to conceal themselves. He restrained an impulse to wave. Security men were notorious for their lack of humour. He turned his attention back to the gate.

A stockily-built man aged about forty, wearing a dark blue lightweight suit and carrying a black over-night case, detached himself from the stream of passengers and came across to Breakenridge. A grin creased his tanned face.

'Still alive, you big bastard.'

'Hi, Sam.'

As the two men shook hands, the tiredness washed away from Breakenridge. Sam Willard was one of the very few people he could call a friend. The bond between them dated back to the early days in the Special Forces in Vietnam, the time before disillusionment, the shattering of bright hopes. Now they were older and one hell of a lot wiser.

In silence, the two men headed for the bar, Sam matching his stride to that of the big man beside him. He flicked a quick appraising glance at Breakenridge as they made their way to a table. A few more grey hairs were evident at the temples, the lines at the corners of the mouth perhaps more deeply etched. Maybe that woman in Paris really had gotten to him after all!

The waitress brought cognacs and coffee. Two men settled at a table some distance away and she went unhurriedly to take their order. Breakenridge lit a Disque Bleu. Sam nodded at the lighter.

'I'm surprised you kept it.'

'Beats the hell out of matches,' Breakenridge grinned.

Sam took a sip of his Rémy Martin. 'Did you know he's divorcing her?'

Breakenridge shook his head. There was a glint of amusement in Sam's eyes.

'The guy that took over your job really did try to knock him off. A car accident. The Rolls will never roll again. And that made the Baron really pissed off.'

'Sam.' There was a slight edge to Breakenridge's voice. 'I didn't get you down here to hear the latest gossip from Paris.'

Sam held up a hand. 'Point taken. What are you into?'

Breakenridge stubbed out his cigarette in the ashtray. 'Remember the team of archaeologists that got kidnapped by Polisario guerillas in Morocco?'

Sam frowned. 'Right,' he said slowly. 'About six, seven months back? A French outfit?'

'That's them. I have to go get them out.'

Sam stared at him in surprise. 'I thought you were finished after Angola.'

'I was. But I don't have any choice any more. I've had my hide nailed to the barn door.'

Sam looked at him for a long moment. Then he said quietly: 'We're sitting in an airport. Let's just get on a plane and fly away.'

Breakenridge shook his head. 'Sam, I'd never make it to the ticket desk.'

'I would.'

'Not this time. The table behind me. Two men. French Security. SDECE.'

Sam blinked. 'Jesus,' he said softly. He had an overwhelming urge to get up and leave. Three years of non-involvement, sitting in the background, setting up operations, not having to be in the field getting his ass shot off had suddenly been wiped out. Now he was out in the open. He felt a flash of anger.

'I'm sorry, Sam.'

Willard looked at him. Then he shrugged. 'What the hell! I did a good snow job on myself for three years. Had to end sometime.'

Breakenridge stood up. 'Have another cognac. I'll be right back.'

Willard watched as one of the two security agents followed Breakenridge from the bar. The other stayed put. Willard called the waitress over.

Five minutes later, Breakenridge returned, placed a cheap plastic briefcase on the table and sat.

'Airport locker,' he said by way of explanation. 'It's all there. Money, maps, everything. When you've been through it, put it back in the locker until your plane leaves in the morning. Here's the key.'

He dropped it on the briefcase. Willard picked it up and put it in his pocket.

'When and where?' he asked.

'Four days' time. Southern Algeria.'

Willard's eyebrows lifted. 'You really pick 'em.'

'There's a good way in.'

'Yeah?' Willard was sceptical. 'Surprise me.'

Breakenridge smiled. 'The oldest trick in military history. A Trojan Horse. But this one's got a three-pointed star on its noseband.'

'You,' said Willard, 'arouse my curiosity.'

Breakenridge leaned forward and began to talk, low-voiced. From time to time he lit a Disque Bleu.

The waitress brought more cognac and coffee. Willard listened intently, occasionally asking a pertinent question and making notes on a small pad. When Breakenridge finished, the two men sat in silence for some moments. Then Willard glanced down at his notes.

'How many men for how long?'

'Eight. Including a second-in-command. The contract is for two weeks.'

'What's the money?'

'Five thousand dollars for each man. Plus an extra three for the second-in-command. You take the usual percentage for setting up the team.'

'How do you want me to set up the payments?'

'Through the "Paymaster" in Amsterdam. He'll collect uncut diamonds for the full amount from a cut-out in Paris the day after tomorrow. When he's back in Amsterdam, he calls you. You call me and it's on.'

'Expenses?'

'In the briefcase.'

'About the team.' Willard flipped to a fresh page on his notepad. 'Anything special?'

Breakenridge took a wrapped cube of sugar from the bowl and set it down on the table. 'A mechanic. Diesel. The best. If anything blows on that rig we're in trouble.' His voice was clipped, incisive. Another sugar cube joined the first. 'Someone who speaks fluent Arabic and knows the area well.'

Willard looked up from his notepad. 'That could be a problem,' he murmured.

Breakenridge grinned. 'You're gonna have to earn your percentage, Sam. Next, I want an explosives expert. And make sure he's not a nut and still has his fingers connected to his brain.'

'That it?'

Breakenridge placed two more sugar cubes alongside the other three. 'Here's the kicker. Two bike men. Off-trail. They've gotta be good.'

'Bike men?' The surprise showed on Willard's face. He'd filled some weird orders in his time, but this was snowfall in Death Valley.

'I've got two Yamaha 125s. My aces in the hole.'

Breakenridge scooped the sugar cubes off the table and dropped them back in the bowl.

'My number two. It's a rough job. He's got to get the men to Oran, stash 'em in the "safe house", brief them, then move them to the pick-up point. Everything depends on that end of things going right. If he fouls up, I'm out on a candled 'chute without a reserve.' He leaned in close. 'He has to be good, Sam. I mean ace.'

Willard poked at the sugar cubes, stirring them with his finger. Finally, and without looking up, he said: 'You've got him.'

'Who?'

'Me.'

He looked up. The slate-grey eyes were steady, expressionless, cold. 'I know what you're going to say. I've been out of it for three years. Am I as quick and as sure as I was? Can I still do it?'

Willard heard the words spill out, tumbling over each other. He took a breath. 'I can. Believe me, I can.'

Breakenridge's eyes never left Willard's face. It was as if they searched for something deeply hidden.

'Three years,' he said softly. 'It's a long time, Sam. A lifetime. I've been out eight months and French Security made me buzzard bait. As easy as that!' He snapped his fingers. 'Three years, Sam,' he repeated slowly. 'Can you get back your edge in four days?'

The question hacked into Sam like a sabre blade. He winced and, knowing the answer, made none. He watched Breakenridge light a Disque Bleu and blow the smoke away. The symbolism of the action did not escape him.

'One mistake, one small error on your part, could snuff out a lot of men's lives. Including mine. And I don't have the time to prove you out.' Breakenridge drew on the cigarette. 'You still want in?'

Willard nodded.

'No favours, Sam. My terms.'

The acceptance was harsh, the future laid out like a railroad track on a bare plain.

'Your terms.'

One of the pair of French Security men got up and went to the telephone at the end of the bar.

'About them.' Willard's eyes flicked to the agent as he inserted a *jeton* and dialled. 'If we pull this off, we'll not only know *where* the bodies are buried, but *who* buried them. And we both know what that'll mean for us.'

Breakenridge extinguished his cigarette. 'Don Tuck,' he said quietly. 'Can you locate him? In a hurry?

'Don Tuck?'

The question took Willard by surprise. Tuck was an Australian, a brash extrovert with a midriff running to fat. The first time he'd encountered him was back in '69, piloting a 'Puff The Magic Dragon' gunship in Laos. A crazy bastard with a penchant for singing hymns and a liking for nubile females. In the air he was a mixture of the Red Baron and Errol Flynn on one of his better days – Willard had proof from nerve-shattered aircrews that had flown with him.

'Don Tuck,' he repeated. 'Sure, I know where he is. Right now he's in Spain. Got his own outfit. Stunt flying. Working on a movie in Almeria. What do you need him for?'

'I'll let you know when the time comes. Just get him down here within twenty-four hours. Whatever it costs. Tell him to come straight to me. The address and details are in the briefcase. Get him or we could wind up dead!'

The West Virginian accent had hardened with insistence. It got through to Willard.

"All right,' he said defensively, 'I'll get him.' He knew from long experience that when Breakenridge was in this mood you jumped, or else . . .

'Anything more?'

Breakenridge stood up and looked down at him. 'See you in Oran.'

He walked out of the bar, tagged by one of the Security men. The other stayed. Willard opened the briefcase and began to study the contents.

CHAPTER FOUR

The sun beat down out of a clear sky onto the white pédalo drifting on the sparkling blue Mediterranean. On shore, a hundred yards away, the citizens of Marseilles sweltered in the mid-morning heat. Reflections splintered off the windshields of cars moving along the Promenade de la Plage.

'I reckon it could work, sport.'

Breakenridge glanced at Don Tuck. The Australian filled his side of the pédalo like a large rubicund cloud, red face streaked with sweat above the vivid floral shirt.

'Gonna cost you, though.'

'Not me,' said Breakenridge. 'The French.'

'Think they'll go for it?'

'We'll convince 'em.'

Tuck reached down into a plastic net bag trailing in the sea beside him and came up with two cans of Coke. He passed one to Breakenridge.

'What sort of aircraft d'you want?'

'What have you got?'

Tuck ripped the tab off his Coke and took a long swallow. He belched, then said: 'How about a Junkers 52? Got the range, performance, right payload, and it's a bloody good machine. I guarantee it.'

Breakenridge thought for a moment, then shook his head. 'No. Too conspicuous.'

Tuck shrugged. 'You'll never know what you just turned down. A plane certified as used by the fuckin' Fuehrer himself.'

Breakenridge grinned. 'What else?'

Tuck sucked his teeth. 'Well, that brings us to the Dak Three.'

'That's more like it.'

'Mate, I gotta be truthful. The old girl's had a hard life. Flogged her guts out flyin' the Hump during the war. Then the Siamese Air Force got their little yellow claws on her. I got her off a cross-eyed Armenian in Egypt. She's a bit like an old prostitute: well worn but capable of giving you a good ride.'

Breakenridge considered Tuck's salty description. The Dakota was a good aircraft and he'd had plenty of experience with them in the past.

'Can she do the job?'

Tuck considered his reply before speaking. A lot of lives would depend on his judgement.

'I reckon so,' he said thoughtfully. 'Spain to Morocco – that's no problem. I can refuel and check her out at Zagora. You think the French can get the Moroccans to go along with the rest of it?'

'I don't see why not.'

'In that case, the only problem is that airstrip. And it's a big one, mate. If the surface ain't good enough I could crack up the old girl on the landing. Then we'd all be knee-deep in the kangaroo dung.'

'If the surface is reasonable, can you do it?'

'Sure. But it'll be straight in, load, and get out. Fast. I got my crew to think about. They come first. Sorry.'

Breakenridge nodded. 'That's fair enough, Don. But there's just a couple more things.'

'Such as?'

'Let's call them extras. Why don't we get some exercise while I tell you about them?'

The water churned behind the pédalo as it started to move across the bay. On the Plage, a man watched their progress through a powerful pair of binoculars. Behind him, blatantly parked in a *zone interdit,* was a Simca Thousand. Inside it, a man spoke softly and hurriedly into a hand-mike. Out to sea, a grey patrol boat hung on the rim of the horizon.

The high-pitched snarl of the Yamaha 125E at peak revs ricocheted off the warehouse walls, and was abruptly stilled as the mechanic shut down the throttle.

'A plane?'

Guillard stared at Breakenridge incredulously, as if unable to believe the American was serious. Breakenridge nodded.

'A plane,' he insisted quietly.

Guillard threw his arms wide in exasperation. 'I don't believe it,' he said. There was a note of near-desperation in his voice. 'Already you have demanded two motorcycles. For what purpose you have not explained! The types of weapons you insisted upon caused us problems. Not to mention the uncut diamonds! Now you want an aircraft. Why?'

'Like I told you when I first saw this set-up, after we hit the fort your plan could go wrong. If it does, we'll need a back-up, another way out. So . . . we have a plane sitting at Zagora in Morocco. At a pre-set time it flies to the border. If the shit hits the fan, we call him in and he puts down at this airstrip.' Breakenridge pointed to a spot on the satellite picture lying on the workbench in front of him. 'Then we fly back across the border, meet up with your people and complete your escape plan.'

Guillard stared at the satellite picture for some moments. He was forced to admit the idea had merit. The time of real danger was after the rescue of the hostages. If, as the American so quaintly put it, 'the shit hit the fan' on their return from the fort, an alternative way out would be essential.

'I have to admit it makes sense,' he said grudgingly. 'But where do we obtain a suitable aircraft at such short notice?'

'That's where I come in, sport.'

Guillard eyed the large sweaty Australian with some distaste. The obvious brashness of the man, combined with his appalling taste in clothes, offended his every sense.

'Oh? How?'

Breakenridge had merely introduced Tuck as a member of his team, nothing more. Suddenly he was in the aircraft business.

'I got a Dak Three. Sweet as a virgin's ass an' just as eager. Right now, she's sittin' at Almeria rarin' to go. Three weeks ago we did a "major" on her Pratt and Whitney's. She'll fly for two thousand miles at ten thousand feet. Straight. Takes twenty-eight people. So if you invite any more they're gonna have to fly on the fuckin' outside.'

Breakenridge watched Guillard's reaction to this with quiet amusement.

'This . . . ah . . . Dak Three.' Guillard fastened on the name, extracting it from the Australian's exuberant flow. 'Are you trying to sell it to me?'

Tuck laughed, a fruity bellow. 'The hell I am, mate. This is a hire job.'

'I see. And what about a pilot?'

'Got your beady little eyes fixed right on him.'

'You?' Guillard could not hide the scathing note in his voice.

'Too bloody right,' said Tuck aggressively. 'Where she goes, I go.'

Guillard looked at Breakenridge questioningly. 'This man. This plane. Your choice?'

'My choice.'

'Then I shall have to rely on your judgement.'

He smiled crookedly. Breakenridge kept a poker face. Inwardly he was surprised at the ease with which they'd got the Frenchman's agreement to this last-minute development.

'Of course, I shall have to convince Paris. But that's my problem.' Guillard indicated the Michelin on the workbench. 'Now show me this place Zagora.'

Tuck's beefy forefinger hit the map, black-rimmed nail obscuring the area in question. Guillard removed the obstacle delicately. The hand reminded him of the blade on a steam shovel.

He studied the map carefully. Zagora was some hundred and fifty kilometres from the border with Algeria, and roughly another three hundred and fifty to the abandoned airstrip. A round trip of a thousand kilometres. Questions formed in his mind.

'You appear to have the range,' he said to Tuck. 'How long will the round trip take you?'

The Australian scratched at his unshaven jaw, appearing to think.

'Four hours. Maybe less. At zero feet my airspeed will be down to about one seventy, one seventy-five. I'll be ground hogging all the way in and out. There's just one bloody great snag though, sport.'

Guillard raised an eyebrow. 'Oh?'

'The airstrip. If the surface is bad it's a no go.'

'But what about the people on the ground?'

'I'd give 'em a cheery wave.'

Guillard opened his mouth as if to say something then,

obviously thinking better of it, turned to Breakenridge. 'What happens then?'

'I'll saw that log if and when we get to it. Meantime,' he glanced at Tuck, 'I've got some things to check over. When you two have finished, let me know.'

He turned and strode to the huge truck, now camouflaged in its new identity. Emblazoned on the flanks of the main forty-foot trailer in bright red were the words: *Compagnie Ligne Rouge.* Below this, a signwriter was putting the finishing touches to a company address registered in Ostend. The rear doors of the trailer were open and a mechanic was wheeling a Yamaha up a ramp into the interior. Breakenridge watched as the machine was locked into position alongside its mate at the front of the trailer. He took a typed list from his pocket and put a check mark against this item.

Climbing inside, he painstakingly inspected and checked off every single piece of equipment. Nothing escaped his attention. Eventually, satisfied, he turned his attention to the draw-bar trailer. This was the one in which the team would be travelling on the journey to the fort. After the attack, they would get rid of it.

Inside, he tried to visualise what it would be like for seven men living in these cramped conditions over a period of days. Even with the air-conditioning unit – which could only be in use while they were on the move because of its giveaway noise – they were in for a rough time. The eighth member of the team would travel in the cab with him and the driver, rotating with the others in here to give each of them a break. Given the circumstances, it was the best he could do.

Sand tracks, light-weight ladders, first-aid equipment, rope, shovels, a chemical toilet, food, water, ammunition, fire extinguishers, personal weapons. As he checked down the list, the space available for the men to move around in shrank alarmingly. Practically all their time would be spent lying on the narrow fold-down bunks. This presented a morale problem which he'd have to solve.

He reached out and unclipped an AR-15 rifle from the weapons rack, right hand sliding automatically into position around the pistol grip, left hand forward and onto the polycarbonate stock, right forefinger resting alongside the trigger guard, butt tucked in between right elbow and ribs. It was an old, comfortable friend from his days with the Special Services in Vietnam and possibly one of the best rifles he'd ever handled. Its .223-calibre round was capable of penetrating five-sixteenths steel plate at two hundred yards. At five hundred yards, in good hands, its accuracy was pin-point. Without any added attachments it could fire a grenade. Complete with a quick detachable bipod and bayonet, the AR-15 was a very deadly weapon. Which was why he'd chosen it over Guillard's protests.

Flipping one of the bunks down from the side of the trailer, he quickly field stripped the weapon on it. He sighted down the inside of the barrel, checked the trigger mechanism, then swiftly reassembled it, pleasurably surprised at the mint condition of the rifle. Replacing it in the racking alongside eleven others, he selected one of a dozen S&W .44 Magnum pistols racked below the AR-15s. It received a similar going-over. Breakenridge was leaving nothing to chance. He lit a cigarette and stood deep in thought for some time. Then, after a final searching look around the interior, he walked to the rear door and jumped down.

Guillard was over by the workbench talking to one of his security guards; there was no sign of the Australian. Guillard handed a briefcase to the man and walked over to Breakenridge.

'Is everything to your satisfaction?'

'So far. Where's Tuck?'

'Outside. Waiting for you.'

'And?'

Guillard seemed slightly ill at ease, fingering the knot in his sober tie.

'I wanted a few words with you in private.'

Breakenridge waited, eyes steady on the other man. He had a good idea about what was coming.

'Your Mr Tuck. Is he as good as he says? Can he really do this job?'

'You don't like him, do you?'

Guillard shrugged. 'He doesn't exactly impress me. Certainly not fifty thousand dollars worth. And that's his price.'

'Mister,' Breakenridge's voice was hard and flat. 'You listen and you listen good. He's got a fat belly, a loud mouth an' he sweats, but put him in that left-hand seat and he'll fly between your spread legs without the tailplane even shaving your balls.'

Guillard started to speak. Breakenridge held up a hand. 'I ain't finished. I'm a pro. I do my job an' I do it good. Which is why I'm still alive. I aim to keep it that way. So . . . if'n I pick a guy, he stays picked. End of story!'

Guillard's face flushed, accentuating the white scar-tissue below the right eye. His hands, hanging down at his sides, clenched. Visibly he held himself in check.

'I also,' he said quietly, 'am a pro, and very good at my job.'

There was a wealth of meaning in his words which did not escape Breakenridge.

'Then we understand each other,' he said.

'Yes.' Guillard looked at him. 'At last I think we do.'

Breakenridge stepped through the wicket gate set in the big wooden doors and shut it behind him. Tuck, leaning against the Peugeot, straightened up.

'All right, sport?'

'I think we got a deal.' He glanced at his watch. 'I'll take you to the airport.'

Tuck shambled round to the passenger door and got in. He sat in companionable – if sweaty – silence as Breakenridge drove.

After a while, he said: 'It's really none of my business, mate, but I reckon you better watch that French bastard.' He scratched his armpit idly. 'He's about as rancid as a dingo's ass.'

Breakenridge chuckled. Tuck's earthy humour was another of his good points that Guillard would never appreciate.

'I bet that bloody film director is wettin' his nappies wondering where the fuck I am,' Tuck went on happily. 'Took the poor bastard up in an old Junkers 88 last week. That upset his sex-life with the first assistant. An' tomorrow, I'm giving him another unlooked-for thrill in a Heinkel.'

Breakenridge glanced at him out of the corner of his eye. 'Don't push your luck, Don. I want you at that airstrip. I got too much riding on you to be let down.'

The leash was jerked. And Tuck knew it.

'Christ, mate,' he protested. 'I was only talking.'

'Just keep it that way.'

When the Peugeot drew up outside the airport terminal building, Breakenridge looked steadily at the big Australian.

'Now you've got it all straight.'

'Right, sport. I call Sam tomorrow morning for the go-ahead. When I get that, I set up my end of the deal. Plus, of course, the "extras". All being well, I'll see you at the airstrip.'

He reached into the back for his bag and climbed out.

'So long, mate.'

Breakenridge watched him enter the terminal, then eased the car into gear and headed back to Marseilles. There were twenty-four hours to zero.

CHAPTER FIVE

Breakenridge slipped his shaving kit into a side pocket of the large travel-worn valise and zipped it shut. His watch showed 9 a.m. At four o'clock – assuming he received the correct call from Willard – he'd be on that ferry to Oran. If he didn't . . .

His hand closed around the butt of the .32 Beretta lying on the bed beside the valise, thumb automatically checking the safety catch. Placing his left foot on the rail at the end of the bed, he slid the gun into a neat holster strapped to his inner calf. It wasn't much but he might need the edge if things went wrong.

He took a last look around the room. Small, plainly furnished in the nineteenth-century second-hand style, it had been a place to lay his head. Now the bill was paid, a cab was waiting. It was time to go.

The lobby was cool, dark and empty as he came down the stairs. Madame Mercier was not in her usual place. A pity. He'd like to have said goodbye to that quiet, sad-eyed woman. Dropping his room key on the desk, he turned. She stood there, framed in the open doorway, backlit by the bright morning sun.

'Your taxi is waiting, m'sieur.'

She spoke quietly. He walked to her and stood towering over her slender figure. Instead of the habitual plain skirt and blouse, today she had on a light-blue cotton dress and high-heeled sandals. Her hair was different, combed to shoulder length. He felt a strange awkwardness, not knowing quite what to say. He held out a hand. After a moment, she took it, her clasp cool and firm.

'You will return, m'sieur? To Marseilles?'

He nodded. 'I'm planning on it.'

She smiled. 'Then there will always be a room here for you.'

'Thank you.'

He walked down the steps to the waiting taxi. The driver took his valise and opened the rear door. Breakenridge realised that this rare politeness was probably due to Madame Mercier.

He looked back. She hadn't moved from the top step.

'Au 'voir, madame.'

'Au 'voir, m'sieu.'

She watched the taxi until it was lost in the traffic, then turned and went back inside.

The taxi dropped Breakenridge at the end of the Avenue Roger Salengro, opposite the Gas and Electricity complex. Waiting until it was out of sight, he walked to Rue Pierre Aumont and then along its depressing drabness to the warehouse.

Inside, all signs of the recent activity had been removed and two men were scattering rubbish over the floor area from a large cardboard container. Only the massive truck remained as evidence of occupation. In a few hours it also would be gone, the warehouse returned to its former state.

There was no sign of Guillard. A guard lounged in the office in the corner of the warehouse. When Breakenridge spoke to him, the man shrugged and pointed to a large plastic wallet on the desk. Breakenridge set his valise down on the floor and opened the wallet. It was full of documents including a passport. Settling in an old office swing chair, he started to go through them.

According to the passport, which had been issued in Toronto five years previously, he was forty years old, born in Medicine Hat, Alberta, a driver/mechanic, no distinguishing marks. His new name was John Shears. He repeated the details out loud several times, imprinting them on his mind.

The phone rang, disturbing his concentration. The guard emerged from behind his girlie magazine and answered it. After a few monosyllabic grunts, he slammed down the receiver and retired into his fantasy world of impossible breasts and enormous behinds.

Breakenridge shuffled through the mass of documents, rapidly scanning entry and exit permits, driving licences, visas, Customs declarations, bills of lading, vehicle registration details. When he came to the end, he replaced them in the wallet and lit a cigarette.

He had to admit that the various departments of the SDECE had done an impressive job in a short space of time. And yet, as he well knew, all it needed was for some underpaid and over-inquisitive petty official to probe below the surface and the whole mission could come apart at the seams like a cheap shirt.

He looked at his watch. 10.35. Still nothing from Willard. Restlessly, he went out into the warehouse and prowled around the truck. The rear doors of both trailers were locked, the lead Customs seals wired into place. If the Algerians were officious enough to want those doors opened, they would see only what they expected to see: domestic refrigerators and deep-freezes stacked two deep. If they probed any deeper, or wanted the side doors of the main trailer opened . . . He dismissed the thought from his mind. There were enough 'ifs and buts' already about this operation without adding to them.

He was aware of his name being called. The guard was standing outside the door of the office, beckoning to him. Inside, the telephone receiver was lying on the desk. He picked it up. Willard's voice came through.

'Copperbeech to Arrowhead. How do you read me?'

'Five by five. Loud and clear.'

It was the pre-arranged call-sign and reply, a relic of their Special Service days. Any alteration in the wording and the deal would be off.

He placed the receiver back on its rest. Guillard was standing in the doorway.

'The phone call. From Paris?'

Breakenridge nodded. Guillard wore light-blue jeans and a denim jacket over a tee-shirt. It was a surprising and unexpected contrast to his usual elegant appearance.

'Then it's on.'

Breakenridge leaned against the dusty roll-top desk.

'Maybe.'

Guillard frowned. 'I don't understand. Your conditions of payment have been met—'

The telephone rang, cutting into his words. Breakenridge lifted the receiver.

'Copperbeech to Arrowhead. How do you read me?'

'Five by five. Loud and clear.'

He dropped the receiver back on its rest.

'Now it's on.'

'Very neat,' Guillard said. 'But totally unnecessary.'

Breakenridge ignored the remark. 'Where's this driver of yours? We're gonna have to move out pretty soon.'

There was a short pause. Then Guillard said: 'Much as I personally dislike the idea, I am the one who has to share that driving cab with you. All the way.'

Breakenridge stared at him, disbelief and the slow burn of anger plain on his face. Guillard held up a hand, forestalling interruption.

'I realise that such an arrangement is not to your liking,' he went on. 'But Paris requires that one of us accompanies you until the end of the mission. Unfortunately, in their wisdom, they decided that I should be the one. So I have no choice.'

The spartan, uncompromising lines of the Mercedes beyond the office windows filled Breakenridge's vision. For a few short moments he felt dwarfed by its immensity.

'That's a fuckin' road train out there, mister,' he said softly, 'not a goddamn pedal bike.'

His words bit into the silence. He was remembering the time before the army. Four years of pushing the big Mack semi across the length and breadth of America. Tooling its snorting bulk day and night along those never-ending Interstate highways: Newark, Buffalo, Chicago, Salt Lake City. Images of the cities flashed through his mind. 'Can you handle it?'

'I think so.' Guillard for once sounded indecisive.

Breakenridge rounded on him. 'Goddamnit, mister,' he snarled, 'can you drive that rig?'

'I've had twelve hours of expert tuition at the police driving school.'

There was a note of defiance in the Frenchman's voice.

'Twelve – Jesus!'

He turned away, registering his disgust. What the hell was he going to do? Abruptly he came to a decision. He faced the other man, took a five-franc piece from his trouser pocket and balanced it on thumb and forefinger.

'Call it,' he snapped, and flipped the coin into the air. Catching it on the back of his left hand, and covering it with his right, he waited.

After a moment, a puzzled Guillard shrugged. 'Heads.'

'You lose.'

Breakenridge put the coin back in his pocket without looking at it or showing the other man. 'You drive the rig to the docks and onto the ferry.'

It was an order. Surprisingly, Guillard accepted it without demur. They left the office and walked over to the Mercedes. Breakenridge opened the passenger door, heaved his valise up onto the lower bunk behind the seats, and climbed in. He put the wallet containing passport and documents in one of the storage lockers above the windshield and settled back in the armchair-like seat. Compared with this beauty, the old Mack now seemed almost prehistoric.

Guillard settled behind the wheel, glancing over the array of instruments in front of him. In silence, Breakenridge watched as he went through the starting procedure with an almost copybook precision. So far, so good, he thought. Now, all he has to do is drive the goddamn thing. He reached back for the seatbelt and locked it home.

The three hundred and twenty brake horsepower diesel roared into life, settling back to a steady vibrant rumble. Two of the guards pushed back the steel-shuttered door. Bright sunlight streamed into the dusty interior of the warehouse. Guillard looked across at Breakenridge.

'Here we go,' he said. Breakenridge flipped down the sun visor and lit a cigarette. The words had triggered off that old familiar feeling in his gut. The waiting was over; the unknown lay ahead.

At various times throughout the rest of that July day, the scheduled flights for Algiers took off from Heathrow, Brussels, Paris, Rome and Madrid. Each aircraft in its own traffic lane passed high above the afternoon ferry from Marseilles. The team was on its way.

CHAPTER SIX

Lars Tornqvist was a very worried man. The day he'd hoped and prayed would never come had finally arrived. They'd laid no undue emphasis on this job. In fact they'd made it sound quite normal. Part of the usual run of things. Just go to the airport, meet eight men off the evening flight from Algiers, transport them to his Adventure Holiday Centre in Dar el-Beida on the outskirts of Oran, then take them to a night rendezvous, where he and they would part company.

In the past it had been perhaps one, two or even three people. A few messages. Nothing that had affected his business unduly, nor brought him to the attention of the authorities. His adventure holidays were well known. All year round, he took parties to various parts of Algeria by minibus and Landrover. Over the years he'd made good money – courtesy of the French Intelligence Service who had provided the initial finance for his business. In return for this apparent generosity he was required to perform certain services for them. In most respects he'd thought himself a fortunate man. Until today.

The VW minibus swerved violently, just missing an Arab on a donkey plodding along the crown of the road.

'Shee-it! Them bastards act like they own the goddamn place.'

Tornqvist glanced at the giant black man sitting in the passenger seat.

'They do.'

The wheel was slippery with sweat from his palms. He was used to the heat, but these men were unsettling him. The sheer muscular bulk of the Negro – Tillman, Willard had called him – was overpowering. Those hands resting on top of the dashboard looked capable of crushing the metal as though it were tinfoil.

A front wheel slammed over a pothole. Somebody in the rear cursed loudly. He jumped as a hand touched him lightly on the shoulder.

'Take it easy, friend.' The American voice behind him was calming. 'You're making us nervous.'

Tornqvist eased his foot off the gas pedal. His eyes met Willard's in the rear-view mirror.

'I'm sorry. It's been a long day.'

With an understanding nod, Willard sat back.

'How much bloody further?'

It was the older of the two Englishmen, pale faced, with dark curly hair that ended just above his shirt collar.

'Only two kilometres.' Tornqvist was apologetic.

'Thank Christ for that. Got any decent beer in your place?'

'Lager.'

'Is that all?'

'Leave it, Hale.'

The command from Willard was crisp, brooking no argument.

The remainder of the journey was completed in silence. Finally, the VW turned off the road and under a stone archway picked out in coloured lights. Tall palm-trees, stately against the cobalt evening sky, lined a wide earth road leading to a number of brightly lit single-storey buildings surrounding a large and inviting swimming pool.

The VW stopped outside a glass and stone-fronted reception block. Two young Arabs in white trousers and short red jackets were waiting in front of the entrance doors.

'Butlins.'

The dark-haired Englishman received a look from Willard that froze further comment. In silence the group descended and followed Tornqvist inside, leaving their baggage to be unloaded by the Arabs.

Behind a reception desk was a smooth, unsmiling Algerian in a light-grey suit. Tornqvist introduced him as Youssef, the assistant manager of the Adventure Centre. The routine of collecting passports, issuing chalet keys, information regarding mealtimes was accomplished quickly.

'Any questions?'

Tornqvist's bald head gleamed with sweat under an ornate ceiling light. Eight hard blank faces stared back at him. Nobody spoke. The silence seemed to last for ever.

'Then I hope you enjoy your holiday.'

Tornqvist heard his words coming as if from a great distance. He felt a sudden urgent hysterical desire to laugh at the inanity. Whatever these men were here for, it most certainly was not a holiday. He turned and met the dark unblinking gaze of Youssef. At that moment he knew that the next thirty hours would be the most nerve-racking of his life.

Breakenridge leaned against the rail watching the phosphorescence gleam against the ship's side as it ploughed across the Mediterranean. Overhead, the diamond-cold glitter of the stars pitted the night sky. He took a last draw on his cigarette, then flicked it out and away into the sea below.

'Peaceful, isn't it?'

Guillard's voice broke the silence.

'The hell it is, mister.'

The Frenchman laughed softly. 'You're a cynic.'

'The way I heard it, a cynic knows the price of everything an' the value of nothing. I'm a realist. War's natural. Peace is the illusion.'

'So! A philosopher! I would never have believed it of you.' Guillard's words were edged with slight mockery.

Breakenridge leaned his weight on one elbow, easing round to face the other man.

'Mister, I'll tell you somethin' I told another man one time. He was another smart son of a bitch who figured he knew all the answers an' most of the questions. In my world nothin' comes easy. Fight or go under. Friend or enemy. Live or die. Play it straight down the middle. That's my fuckin' world, an' no penny-ante words are gonna change it!'

He straightened up, menacing against the night sky.

Guillard stood very still. The tension in the atmosphere between them was an almost tangible thing.

'I see.' His voice was steady. 'Then you have just told me a great deal about yourself. Explained a few things that puzzled me until now.'

'An' you better believe it!'

Breakenridge turned away. He had taken a few paces when Guillard called after him: 'That man. What happened to him?'

The big American's voice floated back through the warm night air.

'I killed him!'

Felix Tillman ran lightly out along the diving board, bounced once at the end, then jack-knifed into the cool blue water of the pool below. At the pool's edge, Sam Willard sat with a can of orange soda in his hand watching the men enjoy themselves. On the grass in front of the chalets the two Englishmen, Hale and Parker, Charroux the Belgian, and the Spaniard Ramon were kicking a lightweight football around. Dieter Bauer, a sardonic thirty-year-old from Berlin, was swimming with all the desperate elegance of a drowning man. In complete contrast to the activity shown by the others, Lachasse, a sallow-skinned Corsican, appeared to be sound asleep on a lounger in the shade of a brightly coloured umbrella. To a casual observer the scene would appear perfectly natural: a group of men from the factories and offices of Europe relaxing in the hot Algerian sun, enjoying the first day of their holiday. At least this was the impression Sam hoped they gave.

He looked at his watch. 11 a.m. The ferry was due in five hours, and that would be the most critical period of all. If anything went wrong, there was nothing they could do to help Breakenridge. There was a day a long time ago when it *had* gone wrong. Then men died bloodily at the water's edge in murderous cross-fire. The sledge-hammer blow. The numbness followed by the blinding pain. The VC calling to each other in the mangroves. Breakenridge pulling at him, cursing, driving him into movement. Then the aftermath. The handful of dazed survivors . . .

Water splashed in his face jerking him back to the present. Dieter Bauer was treading water below him. The German's eyes flicked in the direction of the reception block. Two uniformed men were getting out of a car. Police!

Without apparent haste, Sam came to his feet. Bauer hauled himself out of the pool and walked to a towel. The Corsican was already standing, shrugging into a terrycloth robe. He moved away from Sam, heading for the far end of the pool, passing Tillman who was sauntering towards the police car. The football players, shouting and laughing, were in hot pursuit of Parker, the younger Englishman, who was dribbling the ball in the general direction of the reception block. The team were moving into action, not obviously but effectively, isolating the two policemen.

Lars Tornqvist came through the glass entrance doors, shook hands with one of the uniformed officers, and started to talk to him. Out of the corner of his eye, Sam registered a movement over by the chalets. It was the assistant manager, walking hurriedly towards reception. Tornqvist and the policeman had gone inside. The other officer lounged against the car, watching the footballers.

Suddenly, too late, Sam sensed trouble. Youssef! The bastard had been searching the chalets. But why? What for? What had he found?

He started moving, knowing as he did so that he'd never make it. Youssef had too much of a start on him. Then he saw Lachasse, now on the far side of the pool, intercept the assistant manager who was trying to avoid him. But Lachasse moved too fast for him. With a swift economy of movement, he closed in, slipped an arm around the Algerian's shoulders and turned him away. For a moment, the two men stood side by side. Then they walked towards the chalets, not hurrying, as if they had all the time in the world.

Tornqvist and the policeman reappeared. Something was said and both men laughed. Then the policeman walked to the car. He and his colleague got in and drove off. The men began to disperse, their tension easing. A couple of the footballers jumped into the pool.

'Go keep Lachasse company.' Willard indicated the chalets. 'I'll be right with you.'

Tillman nodded. 'You got it, man.'

Willard headed for the reception block. He found Tornqvist in his office.

'What did they want?'

The Swede held up a piece of paper. 'Shotgun permit. He came to deliver it.' He saw the look on Willard's face. 'Something wrong?'

'I think there is. You better come with me.'

They went out of the office, past the pool and across to the chalets. As they approached, Tillman stepped out of one.

'In here,' he said.

They went in. Tillman shut the door behind them.

'We got trouble,' he said softly to Willard.

Tornqvist paled. 'God! What's happened?'

Tillman led the way through to the small bedroom off the dining area. Youssef sat on the end of one of the beds. Lachasse stood over him holding a wicked stiletto blade, point resting lightly against the Algerian's jugular.

'He got curious.' Tillman moved to the night table between the two beds, opened the drawer and took out a brown plastic folder. He handed it to Willard. 'Look what he found.'

Anger deepened the big Negro's voice almost to a snarl. Inside the folder was a passport.

'Charroux!' Tillman spat the word out like an obscenity.

'But it can't be,' Tornqvist protested. 'I have all your passports in the office.'

'Read the fuckin' name,' Tillman shouted. 'It's a phoney. We all use 'em. Part of the trade. 'Cept we learn not to leave 'em around where any lousy shit can find 'em.'

Willard stepped forward. 'Calm down,' he said sharply.

Outwardly he was in control. Inwardly unsure. It had all happened so fast. One minute everything had been going according to plan; the next . . . He was thinking on his feet, aware that the question posed by Breakenridge was valid. Three years out of operations had slowed him down. Dangerously. Faced with a crisis, the men had acted. Prevented disaster. Moved as a team. That was good, but they'd done it without him. And that worried him. Suddenly he was aware that Tillman, Lachasse and Tornqvist were watching him. Waiting.

'All right, somebody made a mistake. Forget it.' His voice was confident, the words clipped and assured. 'Lachasse, stay here with him.' He pointed at Youssef. 'Keep him out of sight. Lock the door when we've gone.'

Lachasse grinned. 'Why don't I just cut his throat?'

'Just do as I say.' Willard rapped out the order. The Corsican's pale eyes glittered momentarily. Then he nodded.

'Tillman, I want the men ready to move at a moment's notice.

Assemble them in your chalet in fifteen minutes. I want to talk to them. Snap to it!'

'Right.'

The big Negro left the bedroom fast. Willard turned to Tornqvist. The Swede looked frightened and somehow lost. For a second he felt sorry for him.

'Got any guns in this place?'

'Guns? What for?'

'Just answer the question.'

Tornqvist swallowed. He looked to be in need of a drink. A big one.

'There's my shotgun . . . and a .22 rifle. It's all I have permits for. The authorities here are –'

'What about the staff?'

'Staff?'

'Where are they? How many?'

Tornqvist made an effort to collect himself. 'There are three chambermaids. They've gone for the day. A barman. But he doesn't come on duty until five. And two waiters. And the kitchen staff, of course.'

Willard thought fast. Stay or go, there were problems either way. He came to a decision.

'Right. Your people have got to be kept away from these chalets. Can you handle it?'

'I – yes.'

'Good.'

Willard's voice was surprisingly gentle. Any more pressure on Tornqvist and he'd snap like a rotten twig.

'Just one last thing. You'll have to cover for him.' Willard nodded at Youssef.

Tornqvist looked at his assistant manager. The Algerian's eyes were filled with hate.

'Wha-what will you do with him?'

Even as he asked the question, he knew the inevitable answer that would come from the American.

Breakenridge lounged against the front of the Mercedes, eyeing the scene around him. Nearly two hours had passed since they'd docked and only one truck had so far been cleared by Customs.

Now the Mercedes was second in line behind a Spanish Dodge. At this rate they'd still be here at midnight. Over to his left, a line of impatient, sweating drivers queued in the harsh sunlight, each clutching a mass of documents that needed to be processed and stamped before they could leave.

Guillard had disappeared inside the Customs office an hour ago. For the past twenty minutes a squad of uniformed men had been carrying out an intensive check of the Dodge's freight. The rear and side doors gaped open. Some of the contents had been removed and replaced, despite the protests of the resentful driver. One of the officials had silenced him peremptorily, and the man now stood watching sullenly.

Finally, the doors were slammed shut and the Customs seals replaced. The driver received his *carnets* and bills of lading, swung up into his cab, started the engine, released his brakes and drove forward. One of the uniformed men impatiently waved at Breakenridge to move the Mercedes up.

He straightened. There was still no sign of Guillard. If they began searching this rig, he'd have to make a break for it. Guillard would be on his own. As he climbed up into the cab, two armed policemen sauntered up to the squad of Customs men and began talking to them. Against their machine pistols the Beretta would be about as much use as a sling shot.

He started the engine, cleared the air brakes, and eased the giant vehicle to the spot indicated by the beckoning official. In the distance loomed the bulk of the Military Hospital at the edge of the city.

The air brakes hissed as he brought the Mercedes to a halt, engine idling. There was a bang on the driver's door. He looked down. One of the armed policemen stood there, holding up a hand.

'Passport.'

He took it out of his jacket pocket and gave it to the man, waiting as he laboriously thumbed through the pages. Eventually the policeman handed it back, apparently satisfied. Several of the Customs men wandered round to the front of the truck and stood talking. One of them suddenly pointed to the Mercedes and said something to the others.

Breakenridge sat very still, evaluating his chances of survival.

His right hand strayed down to the Beretta strapped to his calf. First shot for the policeman outside the cab. Then out of the door, try for the second policeman, grab the machine pistol . . .

Abruptly the passenger door was pulled open. His head snapped round. Guillard climbed in and stuffed a mass of papers into the locker above the windshield.

'Bureaucrats!' he said in evident disgust. 'Four hundred francs in bribes for their rubber stamps. And someday I shall have to account for every sou to another bureaucrat.' He saw the look on Breakenridge's face. 'Something wrong?'

'No.'

'Then why are we still sitting here?'

'You got a better idea?'

'Of course I –' He stopped in mid-sentence. 'Just drive,' he said wearily.

Breakenridge released the brakes, selected low gear and eased the huge truck forward. The Customs men moved slowly out of the way. Guillard opened out a large-scale map of Oran and its environs and began giving directions.

At the end of the Quai de la Douane they swung left onto the Quai Charlemagne. The oily water of the inner harbour glinted dully in the evening sun.

'Second right and third left.'

Traffic on the boulevard moved fast, cutting around the road train like cheeky minnows taking chances with a killer whale. Slowly, Breakenridge settled into the feel of handling a large rig again, sensing the return of old, half-forgotten skills. Little by little he felt the tension of the past hours easing away. They were over the first hurdle.

He began whistling through his teeth, picking out the tune of 'Rhinestone Cowboy'. Guillard stood it for a few moments, then in self-defence reached up and slid a cassette into the player over the windshield. Edith Piaf's voice filled the cab.

To their right, the sprawling fortifications of the Chateauneuf stared down grimly at the city from its hill. Traffic thinned as the boulevard curved to the right, taking them away from the docks and through the suburbs. Under two road bridges and a rail bridge.

'The road forks ahead. Keep to the left.'

Breakenridge nodded and set the indicator going. A short while later a roundabout showed ahead.

'Which way?'

'Straight over and right onto the motorway.'

For a while, Breakenridge drove in silence, enjoying a brief freedom from care. At the start of the motorway he moved the gearshift into top and powered up the big diesel. Reaching up, he cut the cassette. Piaf died in mid-note.

'How long to the RV?'

Guillard measured the distance on the map. 'At this speed – about two hours.'

Breakenridge reached for a cigarette, shook one from the pack and lit it. As he stared through the windshield down the long stretch of motorway, he thought about Willard and what lay ahead.

CHAPTER SEVEN

It was cold. Breakenridge shivered, hunching deeper into the quilted parka. Somewhere in the distance a dog barked. Faintly, another answered. A car hummed past on the road, some fifty or so yards distant, the twin beams of its headlights lancing into the darkness, heading south-east for Mascara. Its passing accentuated the loneliness of the Beni Chougran hills.

He glanced at the luminous dial of his watch. Ten minutes to midnight. Thrusting both hands into his pockets, he leaned against the side of the main trailer, blending in with its dark shape. Minutes later another vehicle approached from the direction of Oran, the hills magnifying the sound of its engine. He straightened, waiting, watching the oncoming lights. Suddenly, the vehicle pulled off the road, bumped slowly over the hard rocky ground and stopped. The headlamps were doused.

It sat there, engine ticking over quietly. Moments later a torch winked. Two long flashes, one short. He took a torch from his pocket and repeated the signal. The headlights came on again and the vehicle came towards the Mercedes, bumping to a halt beside it, hidden from the road by its vast bulk.

The passenger door opened and Willard jumped down. Breakenridge moved to meet him.

'Everything all right, Sam?'

'No. We've got a problem.'

Breakenridge glanced at the dark shape of the minibus.

'What sort of problem?' he asked quietly.

Willard spoke quickly. Breakenridge heard him out without interruption. He noticed Guillard, standing a few feet away.

'You got all that?' he asked him.

'Most of it.'

Breakenridge turned to Willard. 'Sam, get the men and their

gear out of the bus. Guillard . . . the Swede. Send him on his way.'

Quickly and quietly, the men began piling out, stacking their grips and cases on the ground. The last to alight was Tillman. Leaning back inside the bus, he hauled out the bound and gagged form of Youssef, holding him easily, as if he were a doll.

Tornqvist started to get down from the driving seat, but Guillard stopped him. 'You're leaving. Now!' He thrust an envelope at him. 'Plane ticket and expenses. Go straight to the hotel in Paris. You'll be contacted.'

Tornqvist looked at him, bewildered. 'But –'

'The first Air France flight out of Algiers in the morning. It's booked. Make sure you are on board.'

The Swede glanced nervously over his shoulder. 'Youssef?' he asked timidly.

'Forget you ever knew him,' said Guillard coldly. At that moment, the rear doors of the bus were slammed shut. 'You have a long way to go,' he added pointedly.

Tornqvist crumpled the envelope into a jacket pocket. Suddenly, urgently, he felt the overwhelming need to be as far away as possible from this place and these people. Without a word, he started the engine and drove towards the road. The last thing he saw in the driving mirror was Youssef's face and the dark shapes of the men around him.

Breakenridge watched the tail-lights fade into the night. Then he looked at Willard.

'Do it now, Sam.'

It was an order which left no room for an appeal. Tillman released his grip on Youssef and stepped back, leaving the Algerian alone like an animal at bay, dark eyes gleaming with hate and fear. Willard moved towards him. Lachasse held out his right hand, offering his knife, haft first. The thin blade shone dully in the starlight.

A strangled sound came from Youssef's throat, muted by the gag in his mouth. Before anyone could move, he hurled himself forward, crashing into Willard and knocking him aside. Staggering from the impact, he started to run, blindly. In a blur of movement, Lachasse's arm moved back, down and forward. Youssef staggered, took two fumbling steps, then crashed face

'Well,' he began, 'you've already met Lachasse.'

'The gravedigger, right?'

Willard grinned. 'He's a Corsican. They're great on vendettas, by the way.'

'What else does he do?'

'He's a killer.'

'Sounds like a useful citizen. Next?'

'Your two bike men. Jim Parker – he's the young blond kid. The other is Bob Hale. Both English.'

Breakenridge threw a hard questioning look at him, remembering the last Englishman he'd worked with. A man who had nearly cost him his life.

'What's their record?'

Willard sensed an underlying reason for the question.

'They're good,' he said quietly. 'I've worked them before.'

Breakenridge flicked his cigarette end out of the window. 'If you say so.'

His definite lack of enthusiasm puzzled Willard, but he knew the big man better than to push the matter any further.

'The mechanic you asked for. That's Charroux, the chunky guy with the thinning hair. A Belgian. He helped re-engine those Russian tanks for the Israelis. He comes recommended and expensive.'

'I've heard of him. Go on.'

'Tillman. The big black. Explosives. Was in Nam for three tours. First name is Felix. I heard tell he went into the banking business. The out-of-hours kind.'

The corners of Breakenridge's mouth quirked in a brief grin. 'Well, he's sure as hell gonna hit a dry hole on this run. Next?'

'Ramon. Ex-Spanish Foreign Legion infantry. Thin guy with a Zapata moustache. Speaks fluent Arabic. The last one is Dieter Bauer. Maybe you know him.'

Breakenridge nodded. 'Angola. He was a heavy weapons instructor at the training camp on the Zaire border. Has a good reputation.'

Willard leaned back in his seat. 'That's your team. The best I could get together in the time available.'

Breakenridge glanced across at him, sensing his need for

approval. 'You did fine, Sam,' he said quietly. 'All we have to do now is make it work.'

He drove in silence for a while, thinking about the men penned in the cramped confines of the draw-bar trailer, matching names and descriptions to half-seen figures in the darkness of the previous night, balancing the known qualities of ten men against the overwhelming might of a ruthlessly organised state. On the face of it, their chances of success were minimal. The only plus element they possessed was surprise. And when that was used up – as it soon would be – they'd be forced to rely on their accumulation of hard-won fighting skills to see them through. He was under no illusions as to the probable outcome of the mission, but the thought of turning back never even entered his mind.

The big truck hammered on, overawing lesser vehicles by its sheer brute presence in their rear-view mirrors, forcing them aside and overtaking in a snarling bellow of engine noise and a maelstrom of wind buffeting them from the slabsided trailers. Beyond the insect-spattered windshield, the shimmering tarmac unwound in an endless ribbon through a barren landscape.

Shortly after midday, a battered road sign announced the approach to Bechar. Breakenridge eased off the power.

'We'll fill up here with diesel.' He jerked his head at the sleeping Guillard. 'Wake him.'

The shabby main street of Bechar was busy as Breakenridge carefully eased the giant vehicle through heedless throngs of pedestrians and sluggish traffic. It was tiring work, needing all his concentration to avoid an accident. Finally, almost at the edge of town, they saw a service station with diesel pumps. Rolling the Mercedes onto the rundown forecourt, Breakenridge cut the engine, locked the brakes on and climbed down. While a sad-faced Arab filled the tanks, he checked out the rig. It was stifling in the noon heat and he was glad when the Arab had finished and he was able to get back into the air-conditioned comfort of the cab.

They pulled out of Bechar, picked up the N6 and built up speed again, staying just on the legal limit. It was late afternoon when they reached the junction with the N50 to Tindouf. Here they had to make a left turn and follow the N6 south.

Guillard was driving. As he slowed to negotiate the turn, he noticed a group of vehicles approaching from the opposite direction. With plenty of time to spare, he pulled across. Glancing in his door mirror, he saw the vehicles turn in behind him. A few moments later he had them identified beyond all doubt. An army convoy.

For the next ten kilometres he kept a watchful eye on them. In the lead was a jeep. Behind it were two covered trucks and another jeep. Several times he slowed to allow them to overtake, but they made no attempt to do so. Instead, they sat on his tail, a hundred metres back and matching his speed. Gradually their presence began to worry him. In his experience, army convoys of whatever nationality slowed for no one. Why hadn't they passed?'

He reached over and shook Willard awake.

The American sat up quickly. 'What's wrong?'

'Look in your door mirror.'

Guillard edged the Mercedes out slightly to give him a better view.

Willard's mouth tightened fractionally. 'How long have they been there?'

'Ten or twelve kilometres.' There was a slightly apologetic note in Guillard's voice.

'When I slow down, they refuse to pass. And they keep the same distance behind us.'

Willard studied the reflected convoy thoughtfully. It was very probably a coincidence, nothing more. But nevertheless a set of circumstances not to be ignored. Without taking his eyes off the mirror, he said: 'Build up speed slowly. Let's see what happens.'

Guillard gradually fed in power until the speedo needle hovered on 80 kph, then held it steady.

'Damn!' Willard cursed softly. The lead jeep hung there in the mirror as though on a piece of string. 'Ease off. They're not buying it.'

He reached behind him and shook Breakenridge who was asleep on the lower bunk. His eyes opened instantly.

'We've got company.' Willard indicated the door mirror.

Breakenridge pulled himself upright on the bunk and looked over Guillard's shoulder. 'They been with us long?'

'Too damn long,' Willard explained.

Breakenridge assessed the situation rapidly and reached a decision.

'Find a place to pull off,' he instructed Guillard. 'We'll take it from there. Warn the men, Sam!'

Willard reached forward and pressed a buzzer rigged underneath the fuse compartment in front of him. It was wired up to the draw-bar trailer, and on his signal the air-conditioning unit would switch off, the men remain silent.

A few minutes later Guillard spotted a suitable area of level ground alongside the road and pulled off. The army convoy drove past.

'Just keep on goin', fellers,' Breakenridge murmured.

'Shit!' Willard sat forward, staring through the windshield.

Unbelievably the convoy was slowing, brakelights winking. They watched tensely as the vehicles pulled over to the side of the road and stopped some two hundred yards away. Soldiers began jumping to the ground, milling around.

'I'll be . . .' Breakenridge's annoyance was tinged with wry amusement. 'A goddamned piss stop!'

Willard chuckled. After a moment, Guillard did too. The relief in the cab was tangible.

Breakenridge and Guillard got out. Sam stayed in the cab close to the alarm buzzer while they went through the motions of checking out the rig.

Suddenly one of the jeeps swung out in a U-turn and came back down the road towards them. As it drew level with the Mercedes, it slowed.

Breakenridge studied it covertly. Alongside the driver sat an officer, head turned towards them, dark glasses showing beneath the peaked cap. In the rear was a private soldier, machine carbine resting across his knees. A short distance past them, it made another U-turn and came slowly back. It pulled to a stop beside the draw-bar trailer and the engine was switched off.

In the ensuing silence the cooling noises of the big diesel sounded almost like gunshots in the still air. The occupants of the jeep made no move.

'What do we do now?' Guillard said quietly.

'Go talk to 'em. Find out what they want.' Breakenridge took a tyre-pressure gauge from the toolkit and knelt beside one of the wheels.

Guillard started towards the jeep. As he did so, the officer got out and sauntered towards him. Breakenridge watched out of the corner of his eye as the two men met. There was a short conversation between them in French, the officer asking short questions and Guillard replying. At one point he caught the word 'Canadian'. Then the two men came towards him. He looked up.

'The captain wanted to know if we needed any assistance,' Guillard said.

Breakenridge stood up. 'Thank him for his concern.'

As Guillard started to speak, the officer held up his hand.

'It is not necessary. I speak English.' His voice was quiet, the accent clipped. 'It is not often I have the opportunity to converse.' Breakenridge took a pack of Disque Bleu from his shirt pocket and offered it to the captain.

'Thank you.'

Breakenridge felt the eyes behind the dark glasses studying him. He flicked his lighter into life. The captain touched his cigarette to the flame. As he straightened, he said: 'You are from Canada.'

'That's right.'

'Unusual.' He looked away from Breakenridge at the road train. 'You have come from Ostend?'

Breakenridge nodded. The officer's thin lips beneath the pencil moustache quirked in a faint smile. 'I was there once. It is a damp city. Very cold.'

'It's hell in winter,' Breakenridge agreed. Guillard might have been on another planet, for all the notice the two men took of him.

'The other man. In the cab.'

The question jolted Breakenridge by its casual suddenness. This man was no fool. If there was anything to be noticed, anything at all out of the ordinary, then he'd be on it like a striking cobra.

'One of our drivers.' Breakenridge spoke easily. 'We had a rig break down in Timbuktoo. He's bringing it back.'

'I see. I thought perhaps he was a hitch-hiker.'

'Against company regulations.'

The captain nodded. Breakenridge waited, a cold feeling in the pit of his stomach. All it needed was for this man to talk to Sam and they were in deep trouble. Another American voice would be a dead give-away. He made a mental note for the future to have Lachasse or Charroux up front for the rest of the trip. Always assuming they got any further than this point. He noticed a trickle of sweat roll down Guillard's cheek.

The cigarette dropped from the captain's hand. He ground it out slowly beneath his boot heel. Suddenly he raised his right hand. The jeep engine roared into life and eased forward to stop beside him. He got in.

'A safe journey.'

They watched the jeep pull out onto the road and race back to the convoy.

Guillard frowned. 'Curious.'

Breakenridge dropped the tyre gauge in the tool box and clipped it shut.

'Mebbe,' he said thoughtfully.

CHAPTER EIGHT

Later, after sunset, with the truck pulled well off the road, Breakenridge got the men out of the draw-bar trailer. As he had foreseen at the beginning of the operation, the effect on them of close confinement in cramped conditions was already evident. Any edge they might have possessed originally had been blunted, in his estimation, by as much as twenty per cent. And that after only one day. The cumulative effect of this would be disastrous. Another two days and the team would be about as much use as an unprimed grenade. *No way to fight a war!*

The iron lash of his discipline fell on them with the shock effect of ice-cold water being thrown in their faces. A period of strenuous callisthenics was followed by intensive weapon familiarisation and stripping. He was ruthless in his demands on them, accepting nothing less than perfection. When they thought he was finished, he set them to thoroughly policing the interior of the trailer, digging a hole to bury the contents of the portable toilet and all rubbish, re-racking weapons and finally cleaning themselves up to his personal standards. Only then was he satisfied, dismissing them to eat. As he turned his back on them he knew that their individual hatred had coalesced into one, directed at him. It was the oldest and most effective trick in the book. When the time came, that hatred would be re-directed against the enemy.

Guillard, who had been checking over the truck during most of the activity, was now seated on the ground, back resting against a front wheel, eating from a can of French Army rations. Breakenridge squatted beside him, opened a can and started eating. When he'd finished, he lit a cigarette and stared thoughtfully in the direction of the men grouped beside the draw-bar trailer.

'We're gonna have to change our schedule,' he said finally. 'Move up the attack on the fort.'

Guillard looked at him questioningly. 'Move up the attack? Why?'

Breakenridge hooked the coffee pot off a small spirit stove and poured himself a cup. 'So far,' he said slowly, 'we've been lucky. It's been rough on them riding in the trailer, but from here on in it's gonna get rougher. Especially in this heat. Even with the air conditioning I could lose 'em. Just like that!' He snapped his fingers.

Guillard frowned, trying to follow his reasoning. 'What do you mean "lose them"?'

'It's very simple. Profit and loss. What you've seen tonight is profit. I had to get a hold of them and give them back their edge. Right now they hate my guts. It's what I aimed to do. And I want to keep it that way. But the longer they're in that trailer the harder it gets for me just to get them back to the level they're at now. That's loss. And we can't afford it. I've seen it happen before. Men cooped up in airplanes, dugouts, assault craft. Places where the timing's gone wrong. They get edgy, snapping at each other's throats, organisation breaking down. They're separate, not together when they hit the objective. And that's when it all goes wrong. It never changes.'

Guillard nodded. 'I see. What do you suggest we do?'

Breakenridge stood up. 'Push straight through. You an' me sharing the driving. Stop only when we have to. The quicker we get there, the better shape we'll be in.'

'It will be risky. Fifteen hundred kilometres with an average day temperature of forty degrees. Remember also that we have to stop for permissions to proceed at Adrar and Reggane. And from Reggane we can only travel in convoy over a bad surface that lasts for nearly seven hundred kilometres. Anything could happen.'

'I know it.' Breakenridge swallowed the remains of his coffee. 'That's a chance we'll have to take. The longer we're on the road, the more the odds stack up against us. According to those intelligence reports of yours the garrison at that fort already outnumbers us three to one at least. An' mebbe by the time we get there they'll have been reinforced. Hell, we could stay here all night arguing the pros and cons, but it wouldn't make one goddamn bit of difference. You're paying me to run this outfit. Which is what I'm doing. Get some sleep. We move out at three tomorrow morning.'

It was six hundred and forty hard slogging kilometres to Adrar through the Saoura Valley, barrelling through small palm groves scattered along the road, then climbing up to Col 15 and braking heavily on the long steep inclines down to and past Fort Foum el-Keneg, long abandoned. The windshield was thickly smeared with the splattered remains of dead insects which even the washers had difficulty in clearing. Hour by hour, the temperature outside the cab mounted until at mid-morning it reached forty-five degrees centigrade. The brazen reality of this heat struck them like a physical blow as they got out of the air-conditioned cab to change over drivers.

As Breakenridge settled in the passenger seat, Charroux leaned forward from the lower bunk and handed him a can of orange juice. He ripped off the tab and drank deeply. Guillard checked in his driving mirror, waited for an overladen truck to wheeze past, then pulled back onto the road. The Mercedes picked up speed again.

They reached Adrar before noon and pulled to a halt opposite the fountain in the square. To the casual eye it was a romantic-looking place with its distinctive red walls and buildings. At a glance it resembled a massive fort.

Breakenridge and Guillard went off to look for the police station to obtain the necessary 'permissions' to proceed south. Charroux stayed with the road train to check it over and guard it from the curious.

The wind blew steadily from east to west, raking the fine sand across the road in front of the pounding wheels, hiding the stony plain in an ochre mist. Tiredness ate into them. Eyes were red-rimmed from constantly staring through the heavily coated windshield. Bureaucratic muddle compounded by a surly police sergeant in Adrar had lost them valuable time, and there was no point now in trying to reach Reggane until the following morning. Travel was not permitted beyond there at night.

Breakenridge lifted his hand from the wheel and briefly checked his watch. Five pm. They'd been on the go for twelve hours. It was enough. Especially for the men in the back.

'How far to Reggane?'

Guillard glanced at the map. 'Twenty kilometres.'

'Time to pull off. Look for a place.'

A little while later Charroux said, 'There!' He was pointing. Up ahead, on the right of the road were two big fringed dunes, running parallel to each other, the wind whipping sand tails from their tops. Breakenridge slowed, changing down through the box, carefully easing the Mercedes off the road and onto the stony ground. Between the two dunes, he stopped and switched off. The only company they had was the moan of the wind.

'Get the men out.'

'In daylight?' Guillard stared at him. then glanced sideways at Charroux. The Belgian shrugged. It was not his responsibility. If the Frenchman wanted an ally, let him look elsewhere.

'They been in there too long already. Do it!' His tone brooked no argument.

When the trailer was opened up, Willard was the first out. He took in the situation immediately. 'Move out. Deploy!'

The command rapped out urgently. Tillman dropped to the ground holding two AR-15s. Tossing one to Willard, he started up the shifting treacherous slope of the dune closest to the road. The rest of the men came out fast, spreading in every direction, making use of the natural features of the terrain to obtain cover. Within sixty seconds they were out of sight, gone to ground.

Breakenridge turned to Charroux. 'Check out the rig. It's the last chance you're gonna get before we hit the fort, so make it good.'

He walked over to Willard. 'Not bad, Sam,' he said quietly.

Willard grinned tiredly. 'All things considered.'

'If'n they're that good tomorrow night, we got a chance. Bring 'em back in at sundown.'

That night Breakenridge held a briefing session, the men in a loose half-circle sprawled on the ground, listening intently as he explained the problems they would have to face on the following day.

'There's no way around this convoy system betw and the Mali border. It's a bad road right through of the Sahara an' the rule is no vehicle travels alon stuck with it. It'll be a long, stinkin' hot trip with no that trailer for twelve hours. Now,' he pointed south. down the road apiece an' I aim for us to be there at in the morning in good time to join up with the enjoy the fresh air while you still got it. Any questic

'Yeah, man.' Tillman came to his feet. 'I got me a qu stretched his huge frame lazily. 'It's kinda cramped foi me back there. How 'bout me joinin' you honkies up fi His white teeth showed in a grin.

Breakenridge returned the grin. 'Sorry, Tillman. That redneck country up there.'

'Shee-it!' Tillman spoke in mock disgust. 'Wouldn't y it! I come all this way an' I still get to ride in the bac

There was a ripple of laughter from the team as he sat

'Something me and my mate been wondering about. Parker, the young blond-haired Englishman. 'Been me ask you.'

He sounded off-hand, almost deferential, but it did Breakenridge for an instant.

'The bikes, right?'

'Got it in one,' said Hale. He winked at Parker.

'When the time comes you get to use them. Until th soldier like the rest of us.'

'Oh, sorry,' said Parker with exaggerated politeness. only inquiring like.'

There were no more questions and the session brok the men scattering to their bed rolls and sentry duty. Breakenridge turned in he made a check on the surrounding All was quiet. He met Guillard on the way back in. They w to the Mercedes together.

'This time tomorrow night,' said Guillard, 'we'll be t What do you think of our chances?'

'Mister,' said Breakenridge grimly, 'if it was a betting prop tion, I wouldn't even open my wallet. G'night!'

He walked away, leaving the Frenchman staring after him

xt morning as they drove into Reggane, they passed a disused soner-of-war camp, its guard posts and barbed wire still in ce as if awaiting new occupants. Its presence had a slightly npening effect on the three men in the cab. The town itself did le to raise their spirits either. Smaller than Adrar, it had a onounced air of decay with tumbledown buildings and few parent inhabitants. Little by little the encroaching sands of Sahara were moving in to swallow it up.

'They call this the crossroads of the Sahara,' said Guillard th forced lightness.

'More like a cross between Judgement Day an' a wet Tuesday Pocatello,' growled Breakenridge.

After a moment, Guillard and Charroux grinned and the atmo-here eased.

Outside the long-abandoned Commercial Hotel, its rooms nd corridors surrendered to the elements, was a small group of ehicles and people. A police officer imperiously waved them a stop. As they climbed down from the cab, he came over to hem.

'Passports!' he snapped and held out his hand. As he pains-akingly checked each one for the Adrar Stamp, Breakenridge asually studied their new travelling companions, searching for a possible source of trouble.

Two men and two women, all middle-aged and slightly bewildered-looking, were grouped beside a Peugeot station wagon. They were obviously French. One of the men, red-faced and unhappy, was being lectured by a stern-faced police sergeant over some discrepancy in a travel document. Ahead of them was a Landrover with GB plates. A young couple were poring over a map spread out on the bonnet. The remaining vehicle was an old, heavily-laden three-ton truck with an Algerian driver. As far as he could see there was little common ground between any of them, and there'd be no problems when the time came to break away.

The police officer thrust his passport back at him. As he took it, a voice behind him said: 'You are making very good progress.'

He turned. Standing beside the Mercedes cab was the Algerian army captain, trim and erect in a freshly pressed uniform.

'Not bad.' Breakenbridge shrugged. Where in hell had this guy

sprung from, he wondered uneasily. 'You done pretty good yourself.'

The captain nodded. Minus the sunglasses his face was as expressionless as a flat piece of stone. Eyes like chips of obsidian regarded Breakenridge with a cold stare.

'But then I am not subject to the same restrictions as you.'

His eyes switched away, raking over Guillard and Charroux and then back to Breakenridge.

'We've been pushing it some.' Breakenridge gave the admission an air of apology.

'From now on you will not be able to.' The captain gestured to the other vehicles. 'They will slow you down.'

'Win some, lose some.' Breakenridge dismissed it as being of little importance. The police officer, who had been hovering anxiously in the background during this exchange, moved in and spoke in a respectful manner to the captain. After a few sentences the two men moved off, still talking, heading for a building across the street. Guillard let out a sigh of relief as they disappeared inside.

'Coincidence.' Breakenridge gave him a hard stare. 'Nothing more.'

Guillard looked at him thoughtfully for a moment, fingering the scar-tissue on his cheek bone. Then he nodded.

Charroux looked from one to the other, sensing that all was not as it should be. He said nothing. They'd tell him, or they wouldn't. Either way, it was better not to get involved.

The convoy drove out of Reggane, headed by the elderly three-tonner. Behind it came the Landrover, followed by the Peugeot. The Mercedes was last.

For the remainder of that morning they maintained a steady and sedate pace, dictated by the speed of the museum piece in the lead. In places, sand bars ridged across the road by the previous day's wind jolted suspension systems viciously. For the occupants of the Mercedes it was a boring, monotonous and uncomfortable way to travel. Being at the rear, they collected all the dust and sand thrown up by the vehicles in front. Around one thirty, they reached the remains of Poste Weygand, a group of ruined huts. It was with relief that they pulled off for a break.

Breakenridge watched with quiet amusement as the English

couple took out a spirit-stove and kettle and brewed a pot of tea. Guillard came to stand beside him in the shade of the main trailer. 'How long do we wait here?' he asked.

Breakenridge shrugged. 'As long as we have to.'

He lit a cigarette and strolled casually along to the draw-bar trailer. As he came level with the end of it, he saw a plume of dust rising in the shimmering heat, back along the road from Reggane. Slowly, the distorted, wavering shapes of vehicles grew out of the distance. When the shapes took on an identity, he turned and went swiftly back to Guillard who was standing beside the cab.

'Army trucks coming up fast' he said quietly.

Guillard swore. He moved out a couple of paces, staring intently back along the road. The lead vehicle, a jeep, had its headlights full on.

'Another coincidence?' His voice was tight, controlled.

Breakenridge spoke to Charroux. 'Warn the guys in the back.'

Hurriedly the Belgian climbed up into the cab and pressed the buzzer under the dash three times. It was the red alert to the team. If he pressed it once more, they'd come out shooting.

Breakenridge and Guillard waited, watching the racing vehicles bear down on them. Up in the cab, Charroux waited, finger on the buzzer.

Suddenly the convoy was on them in a roar of engine noise and whirling sand. Then they were past and disappearing rapidly into the afternoon heat haze. Soon they were part of a mirage-like image, changing shape and substance. Then they were gone.

'Did you see who was in the lead jeep?' Guillard asked softly.

Breakenridge nodded. 'I saw him.'

'So where is he going in such a great hurry?'

'Appears to me there's only two possible places he could be headed for. And one of them's the border.'

He left the alternative unsaid. There must have been close to thirty soldiers in those trucks; if they were going to the fort, he and the team could be driving straight into a hornets' nest. It was a far from pleasant prospect to dwell on.

After Poste Weygand, the road got worse, slowing them considerably. From time to time they passed forty-gallon oil drums acting as signposts, the only visible evidence in a bleak and inhospitable terrain that they were still on the Trans-Saharan Route. At the Tropic of Cancer sign, three hundred kilometres from the Mali border, the three vehicles in front of the Mercedes slowed and pulled up in the lee of some big dunes. It was obvious they intended stopping for the night.

Breakenridge eased the Mercedes forward in low gear. As he drew level with them, Guillard leaned out of the passenger window.

'We're going on. See you in Mali.'

Surprised faces were turned towards them. Without waiting for a reply, Breakenridge fed power to the huge diesel and drove on.

It was around six o'clock in the evening when they reached the *piste* leading off the main route to the In Ziza water-hole, some twenty kilometres from their objective. With Guillard and Charroux guiding him, Breakenridge backed the unwieldy road train along the *piste* for a hundred yards, well out of sight of the road beside a low dune. He switched off and sat in silence for a few moments, thinking. Then, grabbing a couple of blankets from the bunk behind him, he climbed down.

'Open the trailer doors,' he told Guillard. 'Keep the men inside and quiet. 'You,' he pointed to Charroux. 'Get back to the turn-off and keep a sharp lookout.'

He headed for the base of the dune. 'Wake me at sunset.' Scooping a hole for his hip in the soft sand, he lay down, pulled the blankets around him and was asleep inside a minute.

CHAPTER NINE

Breakenridge carefully pencilled in a cross on the grainy surface of the aerial photograph.

'There,' he said.

In the dim light of the shaded torch Willard studied the wadi shown as running at right angles across the main route south to the border.

'Can we get that close without being heard?'

'These dunes,' Guillard pointed, 'should muffle the engine noise sufficiently.'

Breakenridge's pencil traced a line from the wadi to the track leading from the road to the fort.

'The road block's fifty yards in on this track. Those four guards are the only ones liable to hear anything. It's a chance we have to take. There's no other way to do it, Sam.'

Willard frowned. 'I don't like it,' he said slowly. 'Why not take them out first?'

'We already thought about that,' Guillard said, 'but unfortunately there was no way of discovering the times of changing the guards.'

'Then this whole thing could blow up in our faces right there.'

Breakenridge shrugged. 'I don't like it any more than you do, Sam. But if you can come up with a better idea, I'd sure as hell like to hear it.' He snapped off the torch.

Willard slowly shook his head. 'You're running the outfit.'

'That I am. Time to go.'

The big diesel coughed into life, roared briefly, then settled down into a rumbling throb. Breakenridge switched on the side-lights, selected crawler gear, released the brakes and slowly eased the massive truck forward along the *piste*.

Suddenly the dark figure of Charroux appeared a little way ahead of them, frantically waving his arms. Breakenridge instantly hit the brakes and cut side-lights and engine.

Charroux ran forward. 'Vehicles coming.' His voice came urgently from the darkness.

'Which way?' Breakenridge called quietly.

Charroux's face appeared at the open window. He was panting. 'From the south.'

'How many?'

'At least two. Perhaps three or four. It's hard to tell.'

They sat, tensely waiting. Forty yards away, the road passed the entrance to the *piste.* The seconds ticked away. The sound of oncoming engines grew rapidly. Headlights speared the night, illuminating the road. Plainly visible in their reflected light were the deeply indented tyre marks showing where the Mercedes had earlier reversed back into the *piste.* Softly, Breakenridge cursed his own carelessness. Those tracks should have been wiped. Tiredness was no excuse for a page one mistake.

Then the first of the vehicles was at the turn-off. It went on without slowing or stopping. Three others followed it and disappeared into the night.

Breakenridge slumped back against his seat, feeling the sweat trickle down his chest, wondering what those trucks were doing on the road at night and who was in them.

There was movement outside. Charroux pulled himself up to the driver's door window.

'Soldiers,' he said tersely. 'One of the trucks was full of them.'

Sam leaned forward on the bunk. 'What the hell's going on out there?'

'They can't know about us.' There was a tinge of uncertainty in Guillard's voice.

Breakenridge picked up the torch and gave it to Charroux. 'Check out the road. If it's clear, signal once.'

In silence they watched the Belgian fade into the darkness. Shortly afterwards the torch flashed briefly. Breakenridge started the engine and released the brakes.

'We're going on.' Willard made the statement quietly, almost to himself.

Breakenridge nodded. 'We've come this far, Sam. The least we can do is take a look.'

The journey to the wadi took an hour. Breakenridge drove on side-lights only, straining to keep the huge vehicle on the marked route. Occasionally the moon broke through cloud and made his task easier, but at the same time increased the danger of being seen from a distance.

At the entrance to the wadi the road dipped. Breakenridge juggled with gears and engine revs, striving to keep the noise down and still maintain forward momentum. Using all his skill, he managed to jockey the Mercedes off the road and onto the stony bed of the dried river course. In as high a gear as he dared, he drove gingerly along its winding length until, after what seemed like a lifetime, the moon-dappled flanks of two dunes showed through the windshield. He drove between them, stopped and switched off.

Guillard looked at him with respect. 'An excellent piece of driving.'

Breakenridge opened his door. 'Get the men out.'

For ten minutes they waited, the team spread out in defensive positions around the truck, watching, listening.

Finally, Breakenridge said: 'I guess we made it.'

Willard nodded. 'So far.'

Breakenridge replaced the Zeiss night glasses in their case and the two men made their way back down the slope of the dune to the Mercedes. Stopping beside the draw-bar trailer, Breakenridge lit a cigarette, shielding the lighter flame with cupped hands.

'I have to get into that fort, Sam. There's no other way to do it. Before we make a move, I must know where the hostages are at and what we're up against.

Willard nodded. 'How long do you want?'

Breakenridge rubbed his jaw thoughtfully. 'I reckon two hours should do it. If I'm not back by then, you know what to do.'

'You taking a back-up man?'

'Tillman. I'll drop him off near the fort. If anything goes wrong, he'll know an' hightail it back here.'

He crushed the cigarette out, pulled on a French Army combat jacket, slipped two primed grenades into the breast pockets and strapped on a holstered Smith & Wesson Magnum.

'Take it easy, Sam.'

'You too.'

Willard watched the big man blend into the shadows. Cloud

drifted across the face of the moon, obliterating the outlines of the landscape. Suddenly everything felt very cold and hostile. He suppressed a shiver.

'Hey man, I know why you're takin' me along.'

Breakenridge glanced at the big Negro padding along the wadi beside him. Tillman grinned, slinging the AR-15 to hang by its strap from his shoulder. 'If'n I keep my eyes an' mouth shet, why I'll jes' plain vanish.'

The corners of Breakenridge's mouth twitched with amusement. Behind that corn pone accent was a very sharp human being.

The course of the wadi took them south. After twenty minutes' hard going, Breakenridge called a halt and climbed up one of the steeply shelving sides to the top. The moon was still hidden behind cloud, blanketing the land in darkness. Somewhere out there in front of him lay the fort. He checked his watch: it was nine twenty-five. The time was slipping away fast. He tried the night glasses but all he could see were vague, indistinct shapes. There was too little light to make out anything more. Suddenly, as if in answer to an unspoken prayer, the moon broke from behind cover, illuminating the harsh desert landscape before him. The reason for his inability to see anything earlier became apparent at once. Stretching across his front was a long, low dune. Somewhere on its far side lay the fort.

He gestured to Tillman to join him. Side by side they ran fast and low to the base of the dune, then made their way up its smooth, shifting flank to a point just below the long ridge. For a few moments they lay there, panting. Then Breakenridge carefully eased himself forward and up until he could see beyond. Some two hundred and fifty yards away was the fort, standing out in bold relief in the moonlight. He brought the night glasses to his eyes and studied it intently, comparing reality with the original army engineers' plans Guillard had obtained in Marseilles from Legion Headquarters at Fort St-Jean.

All these forts conformed to a pattern, size being the only variation. This one, Fort Pierre Bordes, had originally housed a company of infantry and was one of the smaller outposts in the savage country of the Tuareg. Abandoned in the early 'fifties, it was now a semi-ruin. Of its four watchtowers, three were still standing. From his position atop the dune, he could only see the rear wall in any detail. The ramparts had fallen, eroded by time and the elements. Now they were an irregular line of broken stone, standing out against the night sky like rotten jagged teeth. To his right was a heap of broken masonry that had once been the fourth watchtower. He swung the glasses to the left. The still intact watchtower at that end stood out clearly in the moonlight. It appeared deserted. Patiently he waited. Finally he was rewarded by movement, and he knew a sentry was stationed there.

When he'd seen enough, he motioned Tillman up beside him and passed over the glasses.

'The tower on the left,' he whispered. 'Look for the guard.'

The big Negro focused the glasses. After a while, he said: 'I got him.'

'The other end of the ramparts. See where the other watch-tower used to be?'

'Check.'

'There should be a sally port to its left. That's my way in.'

Tillman nodded. Below the dune, immediately in front of it was a large thorn bush. It was the first piece of cover.

'Watch the guard. When it looks right, give me the word.'

Tillman turned the glasses back onto the tower as Breakenridge crouched, waiting for the signal. It came quickly, a sharp tap on the back, and he was over the crest, rolling fast down the other side and sliding to a stop behind the thorn bush.

He crouched there, waiting, attuning his senses to the night. When he felt ready, he moved out, propelling himself over the ground with feet and elbows, using every scrap of cover offered by the hard desert floor. From time to time he hugged the ground, motionless, watching the tower and listening. The fort remained quiet.

Cloud drifted across the moon, shadowing the ground. He rose to his feet and ran the last thirty yards to the base of the tumbledown ramparts. Again he waited. When his breathing had steadied, he carefully eased along the line of the wall to where the entrance should be. A few rotting timbers hanging from rusting hinges were all that remained. Inch by inch he squeezed between them and the jagged remains of the stone arch that once housed the sally port door. He found himself in a short rubble-choked tunnel. Picking his way forward carefully, he moved to its mouth. From this vantage point he looked out onto the old parade ground and inner courtyard.

Immediately to his front was a large palm tree. Beyond, and in the middle of the parade ground, a sandbagged wall had been built in a rough semi-circle. Inside it, he could make out tent tops, seven in number. In the centre of the sandbag wall was a machine-gun emplacement, the muzzle of the weapon trained on a ruined section of the ramparts to his right. Nobody appeared to be manning it.

He frowned. It was an unpleasant discovery. Whoever was in charge of this place obviously knew what he was doing. The walls as a place of entry for his men wouldn't work. He'd have to think of some other way to get them in.

He gained the shelter of the outer passageway below the remains of the firing platforms without discovery. Stealthily he moved down its length, flitting past open archways that faced the machine-gun emplacement. To his right were doorways leading into old barrack rooms and storerooms, roofs open to the sky.

Suddenly he froze. A man appeared out of a doorway ahead of him, walked to an archway and urinated noisily out onto the parade ground. When he'd finished, he went back inside. There was a low murmur of conversation. Someone laughed. Then there was silence.

With infinite caution, Breakenridge moved forward to the doorway and peered round its edge. A small oil lamp was flickering on a wooden table in the centre of a long barrack room. On either side of it were a number of old iron army cots. In a lightning count he made out at least ten were occupied. On the table was an assortment of weapons, carelessly jumbled together. He drew back into the shadows of the passageway. Strike one! He'd found the guerillas. Now for the hostages.

At the end of the passageway was the base of one of the front watchtowers, overlooking the main gates. The gates themselves were no longer there. Through the gateway arch he could just make out the start of the track leading to the highway.

Above him he heard the shuffle of footsteps: the sentry manning the tower. Carefully, he stepped past the foot of the stairway leading up to the ramparts and flattened himself against the wall, considering his next move.

The hostages had to be somewhere on the other side of the parade ground, probably in one of the old barrack rooms. Somehow he had to cross the open space in front of him, pin-point their location, and then get out without being seen. He checked the time. Five after ten. Already he'd used up one of his two hours.

He unbuttoned the breast pockets of his combat jacket, took out the two grenades, flattened the ends of the pins, and carefully replaced the grenades in his pockets. Then he unclipped the holster flap and tucked it behind the butt of the Magnum. He glanced up. The moon hung like a giant yellow lantern, illuminating everything with its cold light. He could wait no longer.

He stepped out onto the parade ground, shoulders slouched, boots scuffing in the dust. Anyone seeing him would probably take him for one of the guerillas – at least he hoped so. He sauntered past a palm tree, forcing himself not to hurry, to behave as naturally as possible. Ahead and to his left was the curved end of the sandbag wall; to his right, the open gateway. Beyond that, the other tower, also with a sentry. Directly in front of him, parked in a line along the base of the ramparts, were two trucks and two jeeps. He kept going steadily, plodding along like a man with nowhere particular to go. Then, with a startling suddenness, a soldier moved out from behind one of the trucks, a rifle slung over his shoulder.

Breakenridge, trying not to appear obvious, altered course to his left, taking him too close for comfort to the end of the sandbag wall. The soldier called out something in Arabic. Praying it wasn't a question, Breakenridge gave him a casual wave. The man spoke again. Breakenridge decided to take the only way out and ignore him. Out of the corner of his eye he saw the soldier throw up his arms in apparent disgust and turn away.

Now he was past the end of the sandbags, in full view of anyone coming out of the tents. It was the point of no return. He felt his heart beating faster, adrenalin pumping through his system. Light shone from a window in the passageway under the ramparts ahead of him. He could hear music coming faintly from a radio somewhere inside.

Still moving at the same leisurely pace he skirted this danger point and made for an archway further along the passage. Just as he reached it, a door to his right opened, spilling out music and light. He pressed his back against the side of the arch, keeping still, hand on the butt of the Magnum.

He heard someone move across the passage behind him and stop. For a moment there was silence. Then he heard a match being struck. Seconds later, cigarette smoke drifted past him. The roof of his mouth was suddenly dry. He kept his breathing shallow. Whoever it was, was standing just inside the next archway. Someone else came out into the passageway and walked across to join the smoker. There was a low mumble of conversation, none of it distinguishable.

The cigarette arced out into the moonlight. Something else was said, then the two people started to move. They came past him, two men walking slowly along the edge of the parade ground. Not daring even to breathe, he stayed motionless. They strolled into his direct line of vision. The man nearest him wore the uniform of an officer, rank badges plain on his shoulder boards. The other was a civilian. They turned to re-enter the passageway some distance in front of Breakenridge. As they did so, a soldier, rifle held across his chest, stepped out to face them.

The officer spoke to him. The soldier moved back across the passage. Breakenridge heard the unmistakable sound of bolts being drawn and a door opened. Then the civilian moved out of sight. Moments later the door thudded shut and the bolts slammed home. In spite of the danger he was in, Breakenridge felt a small glow of triumph. He now knew where the hostages were being kept. The business with the civilian puzzled him, but he dismissed it from his mind. Right now there was something more important to think about. Like getting the hell out of there.

The officer turned towards the tents, his features showing clearly in the moonlight. Breakenridge recognised him instantly. It was the Algerian Army captain from the convoy. He stood there, obviously waiting for something.

The transport sentry appeared, running. He went to one of the tents, pulled back the flap and shouted something to the occupants. Four men tumbled out, pulling on equipment, and ran towards the parked vehicles. Seeing his chance, Breakenridge slid out from the cover of the archway. Diagonally across the passage a set of broken steps led to the ramparts above. He gained them without being seen and went up them two at a time.

As he emerged on the old firing platform, an engine roared. Looking back and down, he saw a jeep containing the four soldiers driving out through the gateway and onto the track. He hunkered down in a pool of shadow and waited. Ten minutes elapsed. Suddenly headlights showed along the track, and a small open truck roared in through the gates. As it pulled to a halt and several soldiers piled out, he saw the captain walk over and speak to them.

Breakenridge rose to a half-crouch and moved away along the rampart. He came to a section of wall which had collapsed outwards from the firing platform. Quickly and quietly he went over and down to the desert floor.

CHAPTER TEN

At midnight the team was ready to move in. Each man had been thoroughly briefed on his role in the attack. All they needed was the word to go. Breakenridge carried out a final equipment check, then turned to Willard.

'On your way.'

Willard nodded, slung his AR-15 on his shoulder, beckoned to Lachasse, Ramon and Bauer. In single file the four moved off into the night. Breakenridge motioned to Tillman.

'Lead out.'

The Negro padded off up the wadi followed by Guillard and the two Englishmen. As Hale passed him, Breakenridge stepped in behind, bringing up the rear. He glanced back and up. From a dug-in position atop the dune Charroux gave him a casual half-salute. The Belgian was being left behind as rearguard. It was not the easy assignment it appeared to be. He'd have to sit it out on his own, waiting, not knowing, hearing the sounds of action and the silence that invariably followed. No one envied him his job.

This time, Breakenridge approached the fort from a different angle, aiming for the corner with the ruined watchtower. Reaching it without being seen, they slipped inside the sally port tunnel. Breakenridge gave them a minute to collect themselves before making the next move.

The parade ground was still and silent in the moonlight. He tapped Tillman on the shoulder and pointed to the passageway under the ramparts on the right which led to the barrack room containing the guerillas. Followed by Hale, Tillman slipped out of the tunnel and disappeared.

Breakenridge made a final check on the parade ground. Nothing moved.

'Let's go,' he whispered to the others.

Guillard and Parker kept close behind him, blending into the shadows at the base of the collapsed rear wall, expecting to be seen and challenged at any moment. Their luck held, and after what seemed like an age they reached the foot of the tower at the far end. Breakenridge handed his AR-15 to Guillard behind him then, step by step, like a cat stalking its prey, he went up the stone stairs leading to the lookout position above. Half way up, he drew a combat knife from inside his jacket. A few steps from the top, he crouched down, listening, waiting for some sign to indicate the whereabouts of the sentry. There was nothing. Not a sound. But he *knew* the man was there, somewhere close at hand. He could sense his presence. He fought down the urge to move. This killing had to be swift and silent. He willed the man to move, to betray his position. Still nothing.

Then shockingly it came. The glowing butt of a cigarette dropped out of the night, landing on the back of Breakenridge's left hand. He flicked it away in a reflex movement. An indistinct shape moved into his line of vision from behind the buttress at the top of the steps, just four feet above him.

Knife arm extended, he launched himself forward and up. His aim was deadly accurate. The blade thudded home to the hilt, eight inches of honed steel buried between the second and third ribs, the man's heart sliced clean in two. At the same time his left hand grabbed the man's hair, snapping his head back and choking off any sound. Carefully he lowered the body to the stone floor, then crouched over it listening. Satisfied that the killing had gone undetected, he withdrew the knife and went back down the steps.

Pointing to his watch he held up a hand, indicating five minutes to zero. Leaving Guillard at the base of the tower, he and Parker made their way up on to the ramparts. Reaching the stairs that led down to the passageway close to the captain's quarters, Breakenridge stopped. Parker went on towards the front watch-tower fifty yards away.

Keeping his movements to the minimum, Breakenridge took six grenades from the pockets of his combat jacket and laid them out beside him. His watch showed sixty seconds to go. Easing himself up slightly, he looked across the silent parade ground to the far ramparts. There was no sign of movement. A faint 'clink' of metal against metal came from below. It was the guard by the trucks. Thirty seconds. He thumbed off the safety on the AR-15. The roof of his mouth was dry. He picked up a grenade.

Suddenly the stillness of the night was broken by the sound of an engine at high speed. It grew louder. Then headlights blazed on the track leading to the fort. The sentry below moved out into view on the parade ground, staring towards the open gateway, unslinging his rifle. The driver of the fast-approaching vehicle began sounding his horn repeatedly. The sentry looked up at the front towers. He shouted, voice urgent with inquiry. One of the tower guards shouted back.

A door slammed open in the passageway below Breakenridge. Boots thudded on stone. The captain, hatless, in trousers and shirt and clutching a pistol, ran out onto the parade ground. He yelled at the sentry. Soldiers began spilling out of the tents in the sandbag emplacement, clutching weapons and equipment and staring around, bewildered and unsure.

The headlights lit up the gateway and parade ground. The captain took a few paces forward, one hand up, shielding his eyes from the glare. The horn was now strident, deafening. Then the vehicle roared into view. It was a jeep. For a split second it seemed frozen in motion beyond the gateway. A man stood upright beside the driver, waving an arm and screaming in Arabic.

As the jeep erupted into the fort, Breakenridge's first grenade exploded among a group of soldiers, killing and maiming in a red flower of searing explosive and flying steel shards. Simultaneously, Parker and Hale opened fire on the guards in the two front watchtowers, killing them instantly. The occupants of the jeep – Willard, Lachasse, Ramon and Bauer – spilled out, rolling as they hit the ground and coming up firing, hosing everything in sight. The driverless vehicle careered forward and caught the captain a glancing blow, throwing him up and back. As he flipped over the top of the sandbag wall behind him, the jeep smashed into it, overturning and depositing a mass of sandbags on top of him.

More grenades arced down from Breakenridge's position on the ramparts, landing among the tents and shredding the men inside.

Guillard saw the soldier guarding the hostages step out from the archway that had been sheltering him, and throw up his AK-47 to fire at Breakenridge. Swiftly he moved in behind him, Magnum levelled, squeezed the trigger and blew the man's head into a bloody mush. Then he dropped back behind the pillar as bullets splattered the stonework close to his head.

On the far side of the parade ground Tillman had positioned himself in the shadows of the passageway close to the barrack room containing the guerillas. Moments after the explosion of the first grenade, four armed men burst out of the doorway. Tillman came to one knee, the AR-15 bucking as he fired two short bursts. Before the last man had tumbled in a bloody heap, he'd tossed a grenade in through the open doorway. With the echoes of the blast still reverberating in the confined space of the barrack room, he slammed home a fresh magazine, stepped to the open window and sprayed the interior. Just to make sure, he lobbed in a final grenade and dived to one side of the window before it exploded.

It was all over, resistance wiped out. Here and there, dazed survivors raised their hands in surrender. A few wounded moaned and twitched, the dust stained with their blood. Slowly and grimly, Breakenridge's men converged on the centre of the parade ground, herding the prisoners before them. Single shots rang out as the wounded were finished off. Breakenridge hooked the AR-15 over his shoulder, lit a cigarette and watched the final moments of the mopping up. As far as he could tell, the miracle had happened. None of the team appeared to have sustained so much as a scratch. He turned to Guillard.

'Let's see what we came for.'

Guillard holstered the Magnum. 'Just remember,' he said, low voiced, 'as far as they are concerned, I'm nothing more than a member of your team.'

Breakenridge drew on his cigarette. 'Mister,' he said coldly, 'that's exactly what you've been right from the day we hit this goddamned country.'

Guillard's eyes glittered with suppressed anger for an instant. Then his lips twisted into a thin smile. He turned, walked to the heavy door and, sliding back the bolts, pulled it open.

'Il n'y a pas besoin d'avoir peur. Nous sommes des amis. Venez dehors. C'est tout fini. Vous êtes libres.'

His voice was soothing, as if speaking to a frightened child in a dark room. There was movement from inside. Guillard took a pace back. The figure of a man appeared in the doorway, and stood looking uncertainly about him. A thin blanket was draped over his shoulders. Breakenridge steppped forward.

'Take it easy, friend. You're on your way home.'

'Home?' The man's voice was sharp, interrogative. He peered at Breakenridge, one hand fumbling with thin gold-rimmed spectacles, pushing them more firmly into place on the bridge of his nose. 'Who are you people? How did you get here?'

Breakenridge felt a tiny prick of anger. 'Save the questions for later,' he said harshly. 'Get the rest of your people outta there on the double.'

'I'm sorry.' The man straightened, voice apologetic. 'It's just that we have been—'

'Sure,' Breakenridge cut in. 'I understand. We don't have too much time.'

The man turned, calling back into the room. Two women emerged into the passageway, one of them holding an arm protectively around the other. Behind them came three men. All were nervous and uncertain as they stared at their liberators and at the carnage outside.

The woman protecting the other one looked at Breakenridge. Thick black hair streaked with dust and dirt framed large dark eyes set in a high cheekboned face that was classic in its striking beauty.

'I don't know who you are, but thank God you're here.' Her voice was low, barely under control. 'These animals—' She gestured vaguely with her free hand at her surroundings.

Breakenridge broke in. 'It's all right, ma'am. Just a coupla minutes and you'll be on your way outta here.'

Willard called from the parade ground. 'All secure out here.'

Breakenridge turned and looked out through the archway. Beyond the collapsed wall of sandbags, six surviving members of the garrison stood alone in a ragged line, hands clasped behind their necks. Lachasse faced them, one hand resting on the heavy machine-gun. The rest of the team stood in a group close by, waiting.

The released hostages began to move forward, suddenly anxious to be gone. Guillard stepped in front of them, barring the way.

'Attente!'

They halted in confusion, not understanding. The man with the gold-rimmed spectacles called out to Breakenridge. 'What's going on out there? What are you going to do?'

Breakenridge glanced over his shoulder. 'That's my business, mister. Keep out of it.'

The man pushed forward and grabbed the big American by the arm. 'What happens here is our business as well,' he shouted.

Breakenridge pushed him away.

'Get on with it, Sam. We're wasting time!'

At that moment the younger woman broke away from the sheltering arm around her. Wild-eyed, she dodged between Breakenridge and Guillard, through the archway and out onto the parade ground.

An animal cry burst from her throat as she ran towards the line of captured men, both arms outstretched, fingers curved into talons. Willard moved to intercept her. She swerved and was past him, running like a creature possessed.

'Grab her!' he yelled angrily.

She was almost at the line of prisoners when Tillman overtook her, one big arm snaking out to pluck her off her feet. She turned on him, clawing, kicking and screaming. Swaying his head out of her reach, he imprisoned her wrists in one of his huge hands.

'Hey, lady,' he said chidingly, 'I'm one of the good guys.'

Breakenridge's voice rang out across the parade ground. 'Tillman! . . . Get that goddamned female outta there.'

Tillman strode past Lachasse, the girl cradled easily in his arms. He winked at the Corsican. 'Some cats is jes' born lucky. Others has it thrust upon them.'

Lachasse spat in the dust. As the big Negro padded away the Corsican pulled back the cocking handle on the Russian-made PK and squeezed the trigger, swinging the machine gun from side to side, riddling the line of helpless men in front of him. When the belt ran out, he stepped back and looked at Willard.

'Ça va!'

Dieter Bauer moved along the line of shattered bodies and fired a Magnum bullet into each head. It was not strictly necessary but the German was a tidy man by nature.

They left the fort in one of the Algerian army trucks, jolting down the track past the remains of the road block wiped out by Willard's section, and turned north onto the Trans-Saharan route. It was nearly 2 a.m. when they reached the wadi and were challenged by Charroux.

Each minute was precious from now on. They had to put as much distance as possible between them and the fort before sun-up and the inevitable search that would follow.

The six civilians were ushered hurriedly into the main trailer where they found fresh clothing, food and water waiting for them. The team stripped the draw-bar trailer of everything usable and transferred it to the main trailer. While this was going on, Charroux undid the sump plug on the army truck and left the engine running until it seized solid.

Finally, with everyone aboard, Breakenridge eased the big Mercedes carefully along the wadi, nursing its great length around the erratic twists and turns of the sinuous course of the dried river-bed. At last it opened out onto the gravel plain of the Tanezrouft, spreading away before them into the immeasurable distance of the Sahara like a frozen grey sea in the moonlight. He gradually fed power to the pulsating diesel, building up the speed as high as he dared, heading roughly north-west. The second phase of the mission had begun.

The first rays of the rising sun fingered the shadows away from the blood-soaked desolation of the parade ground, revealing it in all its silent horror. Above, a vulture planed down on the morning thermals and settled with a harsh croak on the ramparts.

A hand moved beneath a bullet-torn jumble of sandbags, tents and smashed equipment, the fingers scrabbling for purchase. Slowly, painfully, a man emerged from beneath the debris. Eventually clear, he rolled to one side. A cry of pain forced itself from his lips. The vulture flapped skywards in sudden alarm. After some time the man sat up, an arm tight across his rib cage. Blood seeped from a re-opened cut above his left eye. He stared around him, his eyes not wanting to believe the evidence before them, but his nose unable to ignore the terrible stench of death.

Gritting his teeth against the pain of broken ribs, he managed to pull himself to his feet and stood there swaying. Stiffly, walking like a marionette, he made his way to a truck. The hood was up. He peered inside. Loose wires stared mockingly up at him. Water dripped from a smashed radiator. Not bothering with the other vehicle, he walked back to the centre of the parade ground and took a final look at the scene. He remembered bitterly the phone call he had received at Reggane which had promised reinforcements. If those fat pigs in Algiers had done as he'd asked in the first place, perhaps none of this would have happened. As it was, he would have to live with the consequences. It was his responsibility. He would be the scapegoat. But before that happened he'd find the men who did this. Somehow.

A few minutes later, with a full water-bottle clipped to his belt, the captain turned his back on the fort and walked out through the gates.

CHAPTER ELEVEN

Breakenridge slowly rotated through a three-hundred-and-sixty-degree turn, painstakingly searching the distance through the night glasses. There was no sign of life anywhere. He let the glasses drop to hang from his neck by their strap and sat down on the roof of the trailer, legs dangling over the side. Below him, figures moved about in the cold pre-dawn darkness. Murmurs of low conversation floated up to him. The red tip of a cigarette glowed. A man laughed.

He opened the map case, laying it across his knees. On its clear plastic cover encasing the Michelin 153, he spread out dividers, a blue chinagraph pencil and a British Army compass. Then taking a shaded torch from inside his parka, he switched it on and set to work.

Setting the dividers to the map's kilometre scale, he walked them north-west across the map, marking the distances with the chinagraph as he went, heading for the start of the *piste* leading north. Half way along it, he swung the dividers west to link up with another *piste* that would take them some two hundred kilometres to their final destination: the abandoned airstrip.

Breakenridge studied the route he had marked out. It was eight hundred kilometres over some of the toughest going in the world, waterless, inhospitable and totally unforgiving. One small error could cost them their lives, wipe out everything achieved so far. Added to that was the certain knowledge that, before the day was out, someone would discover the result of their night's work, and the hunt would be on. He lifted his eyes, staring out over the bleak terrain of the Tanezrouft. In the east the light began to change. Suddenly, dramatically, the glowing tip of the sun showed above the horizon.

He folded the map and got to his feet. Before climbing down, he took a compass bearing. Guillard was waiting for him by the foot of the narrow metal ladder at the rear of the trailer.

'You never intended going back up the Reggane road, did you?' Guillard delivered the statement in a flat, accusing tone.

Breakenridge regarded him for a long moment in silence. Then he shook his head. 'Never did like that idea.'

'So we're making for the airstrip. Relying on that pilot of yours.'

'Right.'

'You should have checked with me first before changing the plan.'

'Mister, I told you when you forced me into this goddamn set-up that we do things *my* way. I give the orders. You take 'em. You don't like it, take off!'

Guillard's eyes narrowed in anger. 'There will be a time when you will not be in a position to give orders.' His voice was barely above a whisper.

Breakenridge shrugged. 'Until then . . .' He let the rest of the sentence hang.

The still morning air was suddenly shattered by the raucous blare of a Yamaha engine. Hale sat astride one of the bikes, revving it, head cocked to one side, listening to the tone. The other machine joined in. Parker looked across at Hale and gave him a thumbs-up sign. The engines were switched off, leaving a haze of blue exhaust fumes hanging in the air.

Breakenridge stepped into view from behind the trailer and stood, thumbs hooked in his pistol belt, waiting to get everyone's attention. Finally he spoke, voice flat and measured.

'You're all figuring that we hit a home run last night. That it's over an' we're all free an' clear. The hell it is!' His cold grey eyes swept over them. 'I'm here to tell you we ain't even at first base. Last night we were lucky. But from here on in we make our own luck.'

His outflung arm pointed westwards. 'Out there is some of the roughest country in the world. And it stands between us and freedom. By day it'll fry your brains and at night your balls will freeze solid. And sometime today they're gonna come looking for us. Right now, they don't know who we are or where we are. But that won't stop them searching. And for sure a time will come when they find us. An' when they do, we're gonna have to fight. All of us. I got no room for freeloaders on this trip.'

He looked at the four male survivors of the archaeological team.

'Any of you handle a gun?'

The four men looked at one another uneasily, absorbing the implications of his question.

A small, plump, bearded man took a pace forward.

'I am Jacques de Payeux, m'sieur. Professor of Archaeological Studies.' He spoke haltingly, obviously nonplussed by the alien circumstances. 'I wish to thank you for our lives—'

Breakenridge gestured impatiently. 'Wasn't what I asked you, mister. Can you handle a gun?'

The small man flushed. 'I-I have never held a gun even, m'sieur.'

'You c'n learn, Professor. What about the rest of you?'

A gaunt grey-haired man with a stoop, clothes hanging baggily from his spare frame, put up a hand.

'I have used a shotgun. But only for birds.' Lachasse laughed.

Breakenridge ignored it. 'Name?'

'Mathieu Talmont.'

'Well, Mister Talmont, least you're half-way there. I'll put one of my men with you and the professor. Your next thesis will be on the AR-15. How about you, sonny?'

He pointed to a young man about twenty-five, slim, and dark-haired with a straggly beard. Before he could answer, the man with the gold-rimmed spectacles stepped forward.

'Before we continue with this nonsense, I demand to know your qualifications for command. So far, all I and my compatriots have seen you do is murder men in cold blood.'

There was a sudden silence. Nobody moved. Breakenridge's eyes bored into those of the man before him.

'Name?' he asked softly. The man drew himself up to his full height. 'Major Phillipe Matis. Late Chasseur d'Alpin. Those are my qualifications. Now let us hear yours, m'sieur.' He stood, arrogant and sure of himself, waiting for a reply.

Breakenridge inclined his head slightly, face expressionless.

'My qualifications?' he repeated, still in the same soft voice. 'Very well, major.'

Slowly, deliberately, he unfastened the holster flap at his hip. With equal deliberation he drew the .44 Magnum, levelled it at the man in front of him, the muzzle three inches from his teeth, and cocked the weapon.

'You're looking at 'em. Six big fat ones.' He watched the eyes behind the glasses blink, saw the tongue poke out to lick the thin lips.

Matis took a pace back. 'You wouldn't!' The words were almost a whisper.

'I would. An' you know it!' Breakenridge grinned, his eyes still cold.

He replaced the Magnum in its holster and looked past Matis at the young Frenchman. 'Well?'

'Jean-Paul Gabarret, sir. Before University I served for two years in the infantry.'

'You got any objections to killing anybody, Jean-Paul? If'n you have to, that is?'

'No, sir. Not after what they did.'

'Good.' He looked back to Matis. 'Ever handle an AR-15?'

'No.'

'You will. I'll check you out personally.'

Breakenridge turned away abruptly and strode to where his men stood, grouped around the two bikes. 'Ramon! You ride with Parker. Stay one mile ahead, check for bad ground. If you come across anyone, hightail it back to the truck. Lachasse, you'll be with Hale, one mile in the rear. Keep your eyes skinned for enemy. Report in, the moment you see anything suspicious. 'Got it?' The four men nodded. 'Then get going.'

Hale and Parker kicked their machines into noisy life. When their pillion riders were settled, they roared off, one pair east, the other west. Soon they were separate plumes of dust speeding over the gravel plain.

Breakenridge went on: 'We leave in two minutes, Sam. Tillman, Bauer and Charroux in the back, you and Guillard up front with me.'

He and Willard started towards the Mercedes. At their backs

the sun was now a red ball just clearing the horizon. Sam glanced up at the pearly-grey wash of the morning sky.

'How long do you think we've got?' he inquired softly.

Breakenridge stopped, shrugged out of his parka and lit a cigarette.

'Purely depends on how soon someone walks into that fort. The nearest place with radio communication is the frontier post on the Mali border. After that, it's a matter of how quickly they react and where they start looking for us. We've got to travel by day and lay up at night. There's no other way we can do it without risking the loss of the truck and putting ourselves afoot.'

Sam nodded thoughtfully, considering the problems that lay ahead of them. Breakenridge saw the dark-haired woman standing at the rear of the trailer, sipping from a cup in her hands. He angled away from Willard and headed towards her. At his approach she looked up. There was a guarded look in her dark eyes when he spoke.

'You all right?'

'I will manage, thank you.'

Her attitude was cool and distant. He ground the cigarette butt beneath his heel, scuffing gravel over it with his boot. He jerked his head towards the trailer.

'Your friend. How's she?'

The woman shrugged. 'How should she be?'

He stared at her, trying to work out a reason for her attitude. Tillman, Bauer and Charroux came up and stood by the open doors of the trailer a few feet away. He saw their eyes appraising her and, for some unaccountable reason, this irritated him.

He turned on them angrily. 'What the hell are you standing there for? Get aboard.' He threw a glance at the woman. 'You too!'

She stared in surprise as he turned on his heel and walked away.

The Mercedes' big diesel engine burst into life and the wheels turned, taking them westward, leaving faint tracks on the hard-packed gravel of the desert floor. Another day had begun.

The captain winced as a young medical orderly taped up the

final layer of elastic bandage around his broken ribs. Slowly he eased himself upright from the cot, draped his tunic over his shoulders and made his way to the open door of his quarters. He stood looking out at the wreckage of his command. He had not wanted to return to this place, to look once again at the bloody evidence of failure and defeat. But, when the lieutenant in charge of the reinforcements had found him, he was semi-conscious and in no state to object. Now he forced himself to watch dispassionately as fatigue parties laid out broken and mangled bodies in a long line in the shade on the far side of the parade ground.

The lieutenant who was supervising the work saw him and hurried over. He saluted. 'You should be lying down, sir,' he said anxiously.

The captain looked at him reflectively. He was a very young officer, barely out of training school, badges of rank new and untarnished. His lips twitched in a grim smile.

'Lieutenant, whoever did this has not had time to travel very far. They must be found and punished. What steps have you taken to that end?'

The directness and the content of the question clearly surprised the lieutenant, putting him off balance.

He stiffened to attention. 'Sir,' he began, his voice adopting the correct military tone of the training school, 'one hour ago I sent out two scouting parties to search for traces of the attackers. So far they have not reported back.'

'Very well. As soon as your men have finished out there, I want them fallen in and ready to move. Is that understood?'

'Yes, sir.' The young officer appeared uncomfortable, as if wanting to say more.

'Something worries you, lieutenant?'

'Sir . . . Algiers should be told—'

The captain silenced him with a look. 'Algiers is my concern, not yours. Carry out my orders.'

The lieutenant flushed, threw up a salute and turned about smartly.

At that moment a jeep raced in through the open gateway and screeched to a halt in a cloud of grey dust. A corporal leapt out of the passenger seat and hurried to the lieutenant. There was a quick exchange of words, with the corporal pointing excitedly to the north.

The captain walked forward. 'What is it?' he asked sharply.

The lieutenant turned, face alight with excitement.

'The corporal here has found something. I think you should see it at once.'

Ten minutes later, the captain stood on the lip of the wadi, looking down at the ruined truck and abandoned trailer, absorbing to the full the cleverness of the men who had brought about his downfall. He tasted a bitterness in his mouth as he recalled past conversations and recollected the men. The big Canadian, the Frenchman with the scar on his cheekbone. The cool effrontery of them: to the point of offering him a cigarette. The realisation that he had stood face to face with the agents of his own destruction. How they must have laughed at him afterwards.

Anger welled up inside him, blotting out all reasoning thought. If it was the last thing he did in this life, he would find them and make them pay. Slowly and painfully!

As if from a long distance away, he heard the lieutenant's voice.

'Sir.'

His eyes focused gradually on the man's face. He was staring, puzzled and not a little frightened. 'What does it mean?' The young officer gestured into the wadi.

The captain scrubbed at his unshaven cheek, forcing himself to control his anger. 'It means, lieutenant, that we are after some very clever men. But they made one mistake. They left me for dead. And I know what two of them look like. I also know how they must travel. So a dead man will pursue them.'

'Pursue them?' The lieutenant stared out at the bleak vastness of the hot Tanezrouft. 'Where to? In which direction?'

The captain turned towards the jeep. 'Get your men together at once. I will answer your question very shortly.'

Twenty minutes later, at that point where the wadi flattened out into the plain, their vehicles halted. The captain pointed to faint tracks leading away into the shimmering distance.

'Morocco, lieutenant.'

The lieutenant got out of the jeep, walked forward a few paces and knelt, studying the tracks. Then he came back to the jeep.

'How can we be sure? I agree that the tracks lead in that direction, but they could be going anywhere.'

The captain smiled at the other's doubt. 'Just think, lieutenant. Where else could they possibly go? To Mali? A Communist state? Not very likely, is it? To Mauritania? Straight into the arms of the Polisario freedom fighters? Again, not likely. No, lieutenant. Morocco is their only avenue of escape. And we are going after them.'

'But sir,' the lieutenant spoke agitatedly. 'With respect, we cannot do that without orders. We must inform Algiers at once.'

The captain's eyes narrowed. Without speaking, he climbed out of the jeep, took the young officer by the arm and led him out of earshot of the soldiers.

'Now,' he said savagely, 'you listen to me, lieutenant. We are going after those people, whether you like it or not. Every minute we stand here, they get further away. And I have no intention of letting that happen. Do you understand me?'

'Yes, sir, but—'

'Of course Algiers will be informed. You will send two of your men to the frontier post at Bordj-Moktar at once for that very purpose. Also, we will request an air search. But it makes no difference to my plans.'

The lieutenant stiffened to attention. 'Sir, I wish to register a formal protest—'

'Protest noted. Now get your men ready. We leave as soon as possible.'

The captain turned his back abruptly on the young officer and fixed his eyes on the western horizon. Somewhere out there in that appalling wilderness of sand and heat they would meet again, the big Canadian, the Frenchman and himself. And when they did, the odds would be in his favour.

CHAPTER TWELVE

Hale switched off the engine, leant the Yamaha on its stand and pushed his goggles up onto his forehead. He took out a packet of cigarettes and offered it to Lachasse. The Corsican took one, and both men lit up.

From where they stood on top of a rise they could see down into a broad depression where the Mercedes stood. People moved around it, preparing for the night stopover, their shadows elongated by the setting sun. Stretching away to the north and west were the rolling dunes of the Sahara, looking deceptively motionless in the evening light. The Englishman glanced at his companion who was standing with his back to him and looking out over the way they had come.

'Sod-all out there, mate.'

'Not yet.' The Corsican turned to face him. 'But tomorrow, perhaps.'

Hale drew on his cigarette, cupping his hands over its glowing tip. 'You got any idea where the Yank's taking us?'

Lachasse shook his head. 'When he's ready, he'll tell us.'

'What d'you think of him?' Hale posed the question casually.

Lachasse moved to stand beside him, looking down at the Mercedes. 'We've done what we were supposed to do. We're still alive. And we are on our way back. That's all that concerns me. As to what I think of him, it does not matter.'

Hale considered Lachasse for a moment. Then he said: 'Must be bloody quiet in Corsica if they're all like you.'

He went to the Yamaha, jerked it off the stand and started the engine. 'You coming then?' he called.

They roared down the slope, bucketing over the rough surface to slide to a spectacular halt beside Parker's machine. As Lachasse dismounted stiffly, he noticed the grin on Hale's face.

'You coming out to play tomorrow?' The Englishman's grin widened.

Lachasse ignored the question and went over to where Breakenridge and Dieter Bauer were examining an RPG-7 rocket launcher. Beside them on the ground was a pack of six projectiles.

Lachasse dug into his jacket pocket, took out a full AR-15 magazine and held it out to Breakenridge. 'Someone is very careless,' he said quietly.

Breakenridge took the magazine and looked inquiringly at the Corsican. 'What d'you mean?'

'That was lying beside one of your tyre tracks when you pulled out this morning. Hale and I found it as we rode through.'

Breakenridge tossed the magazine back to him.

'Thanks.'

After Lachasse had gone, Bauer said, almost to himself, 'What kind of a soldier loses a full magazine?'

There was silence between the two men. Then Breakenridge stood up.

'That's a good question" he said thoughtfully.

'Maybe you should look for an answer.' Bauer's face was expressionless as he polished the optical sight with a piece of clean rag.

Later that night, having checked the guard positions, Breakenridge made his way quietly back to the Mercedes. As he approached it, a figure detached itself from the shadow around the trailer and stood in the pale light of the moon. Breakenridge recognised the dark-haired woman. He stopped in front of her.

'Something I c'n do for you, ma'am?' His voice was curt as he remembered their conversation of that morning.

'I owe you an apology, m'sieur,' she said softly.

'For what?'

Her head flicked nervously as though clearing a lock of hair from her eyes.

'For the way I spoke to you this morning. Please understand, dreadful things have happened in the last few weeks and I find it hard to believe it is all over.'

Breakenridge offered her a cigarette. As she lit it from the shielded flame of the lighter in his cupped hands, he studied her closely. She had obviously made a great effort over her appearance and now looked a different person from the drawn and frightened woman of the previous night.

The thick hair was pulled back into a ponytail. Her face glowed as though freshly scrubbed. The moonlight accentuated the dark hollows of her eyes and cheeks, the only visible signs of her recent ordeal. He suddenly realised that inwardly she was as taut as a bowstring and he chose his next words with care.

'Where I come from, ma'am,' he drawled, 'it's considered etiquette for a lady an' a gentleman to be introduced.'

He was rewarded by a faint flicker of what could have been amusement in the large eyes. He waited.

'Dumont,' she said. 'Stephane Dumont.'

'Name's Breakenridge.' He put out his hand. She took it.

'Just that? No more?'

'It'll do to be going on with. How's Marie-Claire?'

She looked up at him, puzzled. 'Why is it that you know her name and not mine?'

She saw a smile spread over his face and realised that he had been playing a little game with her.

'You knew it all the time.'

'Reckon I did. But I asked you a question.'

'Marie-Claire? I'm not sure. I'm very worried about her.'

'What happened?' he asked gently.

For a while she stood silent, staring out at the shadowy dunes. The she began speaking, head turned away from him, voice barely audible.

'At first it was not too bad. But then the men who captured us handed us over to another group. It started then.'

She stopped abruptly. He waited patiently for her to go on. 'They beat the men a lot in the first few days. Then one night it happened.'

Again she stopped.

'You don't need to go on,' he said.

She faced him, head up. 'Why not? We live in a world where such things are commonplace. Marie-Claire was raped continuously. In the end her mind snapped. I was luckier.'

'Luckier?'

'I had my husband. She had no one in particular to care for her. And after they killed my husband, I was too busy looking after her to even think about what had happened. Does that shock you?'

He shook his head. 'To tell the truth, it doesn't. That's not to say I don't appreciate what you've gone through. I do. But if you can hold on for a couple of days, I'll do my damnedest to get you out of this.'

For a moment there was silence. Then she said: 'That is not going to be easy, is it?'

He shrugged. 'Never can tell.'

She caught hold of his arm. 'Please be honest with me. What are our chances?'

Breakenridge sighed. She was pushing him into a corner, making contact with a part of him that he had thought was safely under control since that time in Paris. Unconsciously he fingered the lighter in the pocket of his combat smock, remembering.

Abruptly he stepped back, breaking her hold on his arm. 'We got a long way to go,' he said harshly. 'They're gonna throw everything they've got at us to get you back. That answer your question?'

She stared at him, unable to understand the sudden change in his attitude. For a moment she had seen beyond the hard outer shell of this strange big man, glimpsed something human. Then the shutters had slammed down. Once again he was the cold professional.

'I want a gun,' she said steadily.

'Why?'

'Because I stood there at that fort and watched them cut off my husband's head. Because I was raped. And because they are not going to take me alive again. Does that answer *your* question?'

He ignored her sudden antagonism. 'I'll tell one of my men to check you out on an AR-15. If he says you c'n handle it, you got it. Your husband,' he asked, changing the subject. 'Why him? Why not one of the others?'

'Killing him, you mean?' she asked calmly. 'Albert devised a way to escape from the fort, but somehow they discovered our plan and were waiting for us. He was beaten terribly and separated from the rest of us. Two days later . . .' Her voice faltered into silence.

He saw the tears glisten in her eyes. Quickly he lit a cigarette and gave it to her. She drew the smoke in deeply and expelled it jerkily. Gradually she regained some measure of self-control.

'Thank you,' she whispered huskily.

'You better get some sleep,' he said gently.

She nodded. 'You have been kind.'

He turned to go.

'Breakenridge.' She stumbled over the pronunciation of his name. He looked back at her.

'Ma'am?'

'Guillard. He is not one of your men, is he?'

'What gives you that idea?' he asked, instantly wary.

'This morning. You were talking with him. I was inside the trailer with Marie-Claire. He spoke as if he was your equal.'

'Ma'm, we're all equal here. 'Cepting that one. He's jest a little more equal than most. G'night'.

Stephane Dumont slept little that night. She had never before encountered anyone like Breakenridge. Everything about him was strange and incomprehensible, beyond her experience. No other man, not even Albert, had affected her like this. Instinctively, she knew that if they got away from Algeria she would have to see him again. And the knowledge disturbed her.

Propped up on one elbow, the captain studied the map spread out on the floor beside his folding camp bed. The cot was the only concession he made to his injuries, apart from the light canvas half-tent in which he now lay. The only other furnishing was a paraffin pressure-lamp hissing quietly on top of an empty ammunition box: spartan quarters for a man of his rank, but they suited his nature.

His finger traced a line across the grid marks to finish at the Moroccan border. Where would they cross and when? Was there anywhere else they could go? No. There was nothing but sand and hills until they reached the Hammada du Draa with its road leading to Tindouf and the three garrisons along the way. They *had* to go this way, the way he had come, following the faint traces of their passing. Slowly but surely they would be driving into a trap, he behind them and the alerted border guards ahead. Yet he still felt uneasy, remembering the big Canadian. There was something about the man that warned him not to assume that he would do the obvious.

He reached out, stifling a groan at the pain from his ribs, and picked up the tape cassette from the corner of the map. He looked at it and smiled.

'Sir.'

The captain looked up. The lieutenant stood stooped at the entrance flap, extending a cup of coffee to him. He took it.

'Come in, come in.'

The lieutenant showed surprise at the sudden friendliness. He shouldered in like a large awkward dog and squatted in the confined space.

'I have just done the rounds of the sentries,' he began.

The captain waved him to silence. He pointed down at the map. 'This is our position. They are approximately in this place and heading north-west. Tomorrow, with any luck, we will catch up with them.'

The lieutenant avoided his eyes. 'Yes sir,' he said flatly.

'Still doubting my judgement, lieutenant?' 'No, sir.' The young officer shifted uncomfortably, aware of the other's intent gaze.

'Then let me say it for you.' The captain leaned forward. 'How am I so sure that out of all the tyre tracks criss-crossing this desert, we are following the right ones?'

The captain's eyes drilled into the other man. He held up the cassette. 'Because, lieutenant, we found this. And where did we find it?'

'By some tyre tracks.'

'Yes. But *exactly* where by those tyre tracks?'

The lieutenant stared at him, perplexed. 'In a patch of oil,' he said at last.

'Correct!' The captain's voice rose. 'And does that not tell you something?'

'I'm sorry, sir. I don't understand.'

The captain sighed. 'Then let me explain the significance of this find. First, the cassette and the oil are the same colour. Black. Difficult to spot. Unless of course one is looking for something, a sign.'

'But it could just have been dropped there by accident.'

'No! It was exactly in the centre of the patch of oil. Someone placed it there deliberately while the vehicle was stationary.'

The realisation of what the captain was saying dawned on the lieutenant. His eyes widened at the implications.

'At last,' the captain said softly. 'You have it. But don't ask why or who. Just accept it as a fact. And there will be other signs for us to follow.'

After a moment the lieutenant said: 'There will be fighting when we catch up. How will we know which one is on our side?'

'That is our informant's problem. Not yours!'

'But suppose,' the lieutenant persisted, 'he is killed?'

'A hero's death is always welcomed by a true partisan,' the captain said smoothly.

CHAPTER THIRTEEN

The spotter plane found them at midday. They were fifty kilometres from the start of the *piste* leading north, and into the Erg Chech – a region of massive sand dunes that stretched for hundreds of miles – when the brazen glare of the sun on the windshield was blotted out by the aircraft's shadow. The snarl of its engine battered savagely in their ears as it flashed overhead at less than fifty feet and raced low across the desert ahead of them.

'Jesus Christ!'

Willard grabbed at the back of Breakenridge's seat as he peered forward through the windshield. The high-winged monoplane had gained height and was banking into a graceful left-hand turn, the sun glinting off its canopy.

'It's coming back for a second look.'

Once more they heard the rising crescendo of the engine as the plane came towards them. Again it roared low overhead, filling the cab with noise. Then, as suddenly as it had appeared, it was gone. Guillard hung out of the passenger window watching it dwindle into the distance, heading south-east. He dropped back into his seat as Breakenridge slowed down and brought the Mercedes to a halt on a flat, unmarked stretch of sand.

They sat there for a moment, listening to the pulsating throb of the diesel. Then Breakenridge switched off.

Guillard looked at him. 'What now?'

'Which way did that plane go?'

'South-east.'

Breakenridge scratched thoughtfully at the stubble along his jawline. 'Reckon that means we've got someone on our tail,' he said slowly. 'Point is, how far back? Couple of hours from now, we could be on that track, heading north.'

He lapsed into silence, staring out through the windshield at the approaching dot that was Parker and Ramon on their Yamaha.

It was Guillard who broke the silence. 'Surely they cannot be closer than one day's travel.'

Willard looked at him. 'Don't bet on it,' he said grimly. 'That plane could whistle up troop-carrying choppers. If they catch us out in the open and on the move, they'll slice us up like fresh meat on the slab.'

'You're right, Sam.' Breakenridge nodded in agreement. 'Tell 'em in back what's happened.' He tossed the field glasses to Guillard. 'You. Up top. Anything moves, I want to know about it.'

He jumped down from the cab as Parker slid his bike to a stop and pushed his goggles up on his forehead.

'That pilot see you?' Breakenridge snapped.

Parker looked at Ramon. 'What d'you think?'

Ramon shook his head. 'I don't think so. We were on the far side of a dune. He was already climbing when he passed over us.'

'Good!'

At that moment, Hale and Lachasse roared up. As Hale switched off, Breakenridge asked him the same question he had put to Parker.

Hale nodded. 'Didn't have a chance to get out of sight. Bastard came over us twice. Practically took my bleedin' headlight with 'im.'

Breakenridge came to a quick decision. 'Ramon, what's the ground like up ahead?'

The Spaniard grimaced. 'Some good, some bad. With a truck such as this—' He shrugged.

'We don't have any option.' Breakenridge looked at the four men in front of him. The effects of being out under the appalling heat of the sun hour after hour were already obvious. Each man was coated with a film of greyish dust, red-rimmed eyes staring out of a drawn face. He wondered how much more they could take before conditions eroded their judgement.

'That track,' he said slowly. 'We've got to make it. If we push on fast, take a chance, we could be there in mebbe one and a half hours.' He waited for their reactions.

Lachasse lit a cigarette. 'It could be dangerous. We could lose the truck. On foot we would never reach the airstrip.'

There was general assent from the other three. The grey eyes flicked over them again. 'I know it. But if we continue at our present speed, whoever's behind us could catch up. So we have to try. I c'n get some of the others to spell you on the bikes.'

Parker looked at Hale. Both men shook their heads in unspoken agreement.

'Don't think so,' Hale said shortly, not looking at Breakenridge.

Parker grinned. 'It's what we're being paid for, mate. Don't want no contractual arguments afterwards, do we?'

Hale cleared his throat and spat in the sand. 'Let's get on with it.'

A short while later the Mercedes was on the move, Breakenridge pushing the huge vehicle almost to the point of recklessness, shifting gears rapidly to match the ever changing surface unrolling before them. The motor bikes, gas tanks topped up, rode at point and drag. Hale, now two miles back, steered a wide curving pattern, enabling Lachasse to keep a continuous watch on their rear. Parker and Ramon broke trail half a mile ahead, searching out the best route. There was no further sign of the aircraft.

In spite of the air-conditioning in the cab, the heat became unbearable as the outside temperature mounted to the mid-forties centigrade. The palms of Breakenridge's hands gripping the steering wheel grew slippery with sweat as the truck bounced and juddered across nightmarish terrain that its designers had never intended it for. Sam and Guillard hung on grimly. The conditions for those in the trailer could only be imagined.

Their luck lasted for one hour. Then it ran out. They were travelling fast over a long section of firmly packed sand when, too late, Breakenridge saw the bike tracks abruptly swinging away and off to his right.

Desperately heaving on the wheel and changing down, he tried to follow. But the forward speed and the weight of the vehicle defeated him. It slid on in a straight line and slammed to a jolting stop, the front four wheels hub-deep in soft sand. Reacting fast, Breakenridge set the brakes and switched off. In the short painful silence that followed, he reflected bitterly on the perversity of fate. His gamble had almost paid off. The start of the track was just ten kilometres further on.

Sam's lips twisted into a wry grin as he met Breakenridge's eyes.

'You want to back off and try that one again?' he inquired softly.

Guillard unclipped his safety harness, rubbing his chest where the strap had cut into him at impact.

'Now we dig,' he said bleakly. Five minutes later, everyone was out in the scorching heat, digging and scraping at the soft, shifting sand that imprisoned the wheels. It was a wearing and frustrating task, the powdery hot granules constantly flowing back, threatening to re-fill the cleared spaces around the hubs. Grimly and determinedly they kept at it, knowing the penalty for failure.

At one point, as Breakenridge stood up to ease his back, he saw Marie-Claire wandering towards him, a water-bottle in her hand. He stepped out to intercept her.

'Hey,' he said quietly. 'You shouldn't be out here.'

He reached out to take hold of her arm and saw the sudden terrible fear in her eyes. A scream started bubbling from deep in her throat. She spun away from him, about to run. Tillman moved in fast to stand directly in her way, his face splitting into a wide grin.

'Little lady,' he murmured reprovingly, 'I keep tellin' you us is the good guys. The ones with the white hats.'

She stared up at him, unmoving, perhaps remembering. Then he gathered her up like a tired child, her face close to his.

'Gonna put you in a place outta that ol' sun.' He moved past Breakenridge, winking at him as he did so, and placed her gently on the driving seat in the cab. 'Be back for you when it's time to go.'

As he turned, he saw Breakenridge looking at him. He shrugged massive shoulders. 'Guess I been elected.'

He saw the other's head lift suddenly into a listening attitude.

'What is it, man?' he asked softly.

'Goddamn it to hell! The plane! It's coming back.'

Then Breakenridge was shouting: 'Everybody. Inside the truck. On the double. Move it!'

Faces turned towards him. Here and there his men were scrambling to their feet, automatically reacting to the urgent command. Tillman whirled and, sweeping Marie-Claire from the driving cab, made for the rear.

Breakenridge ploughed in among the confused civilians, hauling them to their feet, shoving them to the back of the trailer, infecting them with his own sense of urgency. The sound of the approaching aircraft could now be heard by everyone.

As the last man climbed into the trailer, Willard slammed one of the doors shut and hauled himself aboard. Breakenridge, about to follow him, glimpsed a movement out of the corner of his eye.

'Matis,' he yelled. 'Get your ass back here.' The man was kneeling in the sand by the front wheel. He looked up.

'My glasses,' he called. 'I can't find them.'

The sound of the aircraft engine was now much louder. Breakenridge swore vividly, swung his door closed and started running. Then he was in the soft sand alongside the kneeling Matis and grabbed him, hauling him bodily away from the front wheel.

The aircraft was now almost upon them. Bundling the protesting Frenchman underneath the main body of the trailer, he threw himself on top of him, pressing him into the sand.

Then suddenly the racket of the aero engine blasted at their eardrums as the plane whipped over the crest of the nearest dune and skimmed across the roof of the Mercedes, the prop wash leaving whirling sand devils in its wake.

Breakenridge heard the engine note sharpen as it turned and came back, again roaring low overhead. It made two more passes, then flew away, its sound dying into nothing. He rolled clear of the chassis, stood up and listened for a moment, then went to the front wheel. Something glinted in the sun. He stooped and picked up a pair of gold-rimmed spectacles.

'My glasses.'

He turned. Matis was standing a few paces away, hand extended. Breakenridge slowly swung them by one earpiece.

'Mister, for an ex-army man you're a mite too careless.'

He saw a strange expression wash briefly over the other's face. Snapping the glasses shut, he tossed them towards Matis, who caught them and hurriedly put them on. Something about the incident nagged at the back of Breakenridge's mind but he pushed it aside. There was a lot to do and time was running out on them.

The captain and the lieutenant stood watching the army spotter plane circling above them. The soldiers waited patiently by the trucks. Suddenly the pilot changed direction, swooping down towards them. As the aircraft flattened out of its dive, something dropped away from the starboard side of the cabin and plummeted to the ground.

A soldier raced out, picked it up and brought it across to the captain. He snatched it impatiently, unscrewing the top of the metal cylinder and pulling out the message from inside.

A smile spread over his face as he scanned the few hurriedly-written lines.

'We have them!' There was a tone of suppressed excitement in his voice. 'They're on foot. The truck is bogged down and abandoned. Check this map reference, lieutenant.' He thrust the message at him. 'I want to know exactly how far ahead they are.'

Swinging round, he began bawling orders, galvanising the waiting soldiers into movement.

Minutes later, the four Soviet-made ZIL-157 troop carriers followed in the wake of the fast-moving jeep as it headed north-west. In the distance, the plane dwindled to a speck in the sky and flew back to its airfield at Adrar.

It had taken two hours of back-breaking toil, but at last the wheels were free of the clinging sand. Now the last and most crucial stage had arrived. The sand ladders had to be laid behind the wheels and the unwieldy vehicle reversed onto the harder surface.

Breakenridge supervised the positioning of the light metal tracks. When finally he was satisfied, he waved everyone away and hauled himself grimly up into the cab. So far as he was concerned, this was a one-shot operation. It had to work. They weren't up to another attempt at digging out – even assuming they had the time.

As he reached for the ignition, a light flashed in the large door mirror. He stared at it, unable to comprehend, his mind dulled by the hours of labour in the blinding heat. It flashed again and again, like a warning signal. Suddenly it hit him.

He leapt down from the cab, eyes staring to the south-east. Then he heard the high-pitched snarl of the oncoming Yamaha, buzzing like an angry bee in the hot still air. His eyes strained for the first sight of it.

Suddenly it was upon them, skittering madly down the steeply sloping side of a big dune. Parker, his long blond hair streaming out behind him, fought the machine at suicidal speed down to the desert floor, then gunned it towards the Mercedes, headlight full on.

He pulled the machine to a sliding halt in a spray of sand a few feet from Breakenridge.

'Something's coming,' he panted.

'How far back?'

Parker sucked in air. 'Ten or twelve miles. Couldn't make out any details. Not even with the "bins". But whatever it is, it's kicking up a bloody great dust cloud.'

Breakenridge glanced at his watch, his mind racing, calculating, estimating the options. There was only one course of action that made sense in the circumstances. If they were going to get away with it, they'd have to move right now.

The jeep, followed by the ZIL-157s, nosed cautiously between towering sand dunes. Slowly, the view ahead opened out. The captain raised his arm and the convoy ground to a halt, motors ticking over. Raising his binoculars to his eyes, he carefully surveyed the scene in front of him.

To the right and left, lines of gigantic dunes lifted their crests to the brassy sky, creating the effect of a long valley. At its far end were more dunes, cutting across at right angles. Some two hundred metres short of this point was the Mercedes, silent and abandoned, the closed doors of the trailer facing him.

He passed the binoculars over to the lieutenant and lit a cigarette, patiently waiting as the young officer studied the situation.

'Well?'

'There is no sign of life, and tracks of a large group of people lead off to the west. Obviously they have abandoned their vehicle for some reason.' He lowered the glasses. 'Engine trouble perhaps.'

The captain nodded in agreement and turned to the sergeant sitting behind him.

'Take a section of men forward. Signal me when you are satisfied that the area is clear.'

The sergeant clambered out of the jeep, ran to the nearest truck and jumped up onto the running board.

As the vehicle snorted past him, the faint sense of unease that the captain had felt for the past few minutes solidified into a definite feeling of disquiet. Although he had made contact with the enemy at last, there was something wrong . . . something he had overlooked.

He stared at the abandoned Mercedes once more, searching for the answer. What was it? It had to be there.

Suddenly, there it was, staring him in the face. Closed doors! He stood up, mouth opened to scream a warning. But it was too late.

The trailer doors crashed open. Bauer was down on one knee, RPG-7 locked firmly on his shoulder, right eye pressed against the optical sight. Smoothly aligning the weapon on the approaching ZIL, he squeezed the trigger.

There was a 'whoosh' as the projectile left the muzzle, then a burst of flame as the internal rocket ignited, sending the warhead in a flat trajectory through the windshield. Neatly removing the driver's head, it struck the back of the cab and exploded. A ball of flame seared through the canvas-covered rear of the truck, incinerating the soldiers inside. An instant later the petrol tank exploded, blowing the ZIL apart.

Beside Bauer stood Guillard, feet braced apart, an AR-15 at his shoulder. He squeezed off a full magazine in the direction of the Algerians. Without waiting for the results, he and Bauer leapt from the trailer. Guillard ran to the driver's cab as Bauer dived for cover at the base of the nearest dune. He had barely reached it when the big diesel roared into life, and the Mercedes began to move.

Stunned by the savagery of the unexpected attack, the captain sat, frozen for a moment in his seat. Then he was moving, shoving the dead body of his driver aside and grabbing the man's AK-47, sending a wild burst after the disappearing Mercedes. Behind him, men began to spill out of the parked trucks, like ants from a disturbed nest.

Before they could collect their wits, they were hit, again from an entirely unexpected quarter. Over the top of a high dune to their left sailed the two Yamahas. They bucketed down the steep slope in line ahead, Hale leading, Lachasse hosing the bewildered soldiers with short burst from his AR-15. On the second Yamaha Ramon, knees clamped hard against Parker's thighs, tossed grenades among the now panicking enemy. Then the machines were wheeling away, engines snarling as their riders powered them out of sight. Behind them they left a scene of chaos, dead and wounded soldiers littering the ground, a pyre of smoke billowing up into the heat-laden air from a fiercely burning truck.

Dazed and horror-struck, the lieutenant rose to his feet, staring in disbelief at what, five minutes ago, had been an efficient, unified command. His eyes met those of the captain who was hauling himself upright beside the jeep, a machine-pistol clutched in his hand. As he opened his mouth to speak, the flames consuming the burning truck reached its petrol tank, and it blew up with a thunderous roar, the force of the blast throwing both men to the ground.

At that instant, as if driving home the final nail in their coffin, streams of steel-jacketed slugs ripped into the survivors, sending them clawing for cover. Lines of bullets stitched crazy patterns across the sand, seeking out metal and flesh indiscriminately. Then, shockingly, it was silent.

Below the crest of a high dune, Breakenridge slapped home a fresh magazine and motioned to Willard, Tillman and Charroux to get going. Weapons clutched across their chests, the four men slipped and slithered down through the soft, treacherous sand. At the foot of the dune they broke into a shuffing run. As they rounded the base of another, smaller dune, Bauer rose to his feet, clutching the RPG-7, and joined them. The five ran to the waiting Mercedes, Tillman, Bauer and Charroux hauling themselves into the back as Breakenridge and Willard made for the cab.

'Let's get the hell outta' here,' Breakenridge snapped.

As the Mercedes lurched forward, the Yamahas whipped ahead like unleashed eager hounds. Above the dunes a pillar of black oily smoke showed their passing.

CHAPTER FOURTEEN

Stephane tucked the coarse grey blanket around Marie-Claire, and stood looking down at her. The drug-induced sleep had wiped the face clear of all pain and fear, leaving a child-like innocence in their stead. For a few hours at least, the girl would be locked in the dark warm cocoon of another world.

Stephane sighed and moved quietly to the open doors of the trailer. A few yards away, figures stood around a small fire, its flickering light casting strange shadows on the night-cold sand. Jumping down to the ground, she walked over to the fire. One of the figures turned at her approach. It was Jean-Paul, his slim figure huddled into a blanket.

'How is she?' he asked quietly.

Stephane shrugged. 'Sleeping.'

Professor de Payeux lifted the coffee pot from a small spirit stove, poured out a cup and handed it to her. She drank it gratefully, the hot black liquid helping to ease the cold chill of the night.

'Poor child,' he murmured. 'I doubt her mind will ever be the same again.'

She accepted a cigarette from Jean-Paul and drew nervously on it. 'Can't we talk about something else?' she said sharply. She saw the hurt look on de Payeux's face and bit her lip. She had not meant to rebuff him, but the events of the past few weeks had stretched her nerves to the limit.

Her hand reached out and touched his arm. 'I'm sorry.'

The tubby little man, looking slightly ridiculous in a combat jacket that was several sizes too large for him, patted her hand comfortingly.

'I understand, my dear.'

'At least, Madame Dumont, *your* mind has not been affected by the experience,' Matis said smoothly.

She looked across at the man facing her on the other side of the fire, its small flames reflecting strangely off the gold-rimmed glasses that hid the eyes behind them. She had never liked him, never trusted him, not since their first meeting in Paris when Albert had told her that he was taking over as business manager for the expedition. There was a coldness about Matis, a feeling that something essential was lacking in the man. For her husband's sake she had tried to get along with him, but without success.

And there was something else: the feeling that Phillipe Matis was using them for some purpose of his own. And now this thinly-veiled insult directed at her, slicing into her painfully erected defences. She stiffened in sudden anger, determined not to back off as she had done so many times in the past.

'My experience? What would *you* know about such an experience?' There was cold loathing in her voice. 'At least those animals took their pleasure in me at first hand. Unlike you, *major!* Secretly, and in your mind!'

The hot coffee hit Matis full in the face. As he staggered back, cursing, hands to his eyes, Stephane spun on her heel and walked blindly away from the circle of the firelight, tears streaming down her face.

Without warning, a figure materialised out of the darkness in front of her. As she tried to push past, her arm was held in a firm grip.

'What th' hell's goin' on here?'

Breakenridge, his voice roughened by tiredness, pulled her round to face him. Unable to speak, she fell against him, face buried in the coarse material of the combat jacket, her body shaking with harsh sobs.

'Hey,' he said awkwardly. 'What's wrong?' He felt her fingers digging into his back, holding onto him as if desperately seeking support. Totally unprepared for anything like this, he could only try to calm her.

Gently stroking her hair, he waited. Eventually the crying lessened then stopped. She moved back a little, her face averted.

'Thank you,' she whispered.

He said nothing, but kept watching her.

Finally she lifted her head to look up at him. 'I think perhaps

I should have cried a long time ago.' She attempted a smile. 'Forgive me.'

'You're welcome.' He dug a crumpled pack of cigarettes from his pocket and offered it to her. She shook her head. He took one himself and lit it. In the light of the flame she saw the drawn face, lines of tiredness etched deep around the eyes and at the corners of the mouth. She suddenly realised the dreadful burden this man was carrying, and how much each and every one of them depended upon him.

'All right now?' he asked her.

She nodded. 'It won't happen again.'

'Don't bet on it.' He grinned. 'G'night.'

He started to move away from her.

'Breakenridge,' she said softly. He stopped and turned towards her. Quickly, she reached up and kissed him.

'Good night.'

He stared after her as she went back towards the trailer.

'Well, I'll be damned,' he murmured to himself.

The captain watched impassively as the final spadeful of sand was thrown on the last grave. He came to attention, hand to the peak of his cap in salute, staring down the long line of humps, each one containing a ponchoed corpse. It was an eerie scene, lit by truck headlights and flickering oil-lamps that cast wavering shadows around the surviving soldiers as they stood paying silent tribute to the fallen.

The captain lowered his arm, gave the command to dismiss, and turned to the silent officer beside him.

'At first light,' he said harshly, 'you will take one truck with the wounded back to Reggane. I am going on with the rest of the men.'

The lieutenant stared at him in anger and disbelief, fists clenched tightly by his sides.

'You cannot,' he gritted. 'Not after what has happened here today. We must all of us return. Others can continue the pursuit.'

'Lieutenant!' The captain's eyes blazed in anger. 'You have your orders. Carry them out. If you wish to register yet another of your protests, you can do so in Reggane.'

The lieutenant flung out an arm, pointing. 'And how many

of the wounded will still be alive when we reach there? Our medical orderly is dead. Do you expect those men to attend to each other?'

'That, lieutenant, is the chance we must take as soldiers. Carry on. I'll see you before you leave in the morning.'

He returned the other's stiff salute and went to his bedroll spread out alongside the jeep. For a long time he lay awake, staring up at the stars. Somewhere out there in that wilderness of sand was the big man, the one he instinctively knew was responsible for everything that had happened. He vowed once again to find him and destroy him. Even if it cost him his own life.

Just after first light, Breakenridge walked away from the Mercedes along the rutted surface of the sand-blown *piste*. At the point where it skirted a dune, he came upon Tillman, hunkered down, eyes gazing northwards.

'Anything?' he asked quietly, proffering the mug of coffee he'd brought with him.

The big Negro gulped at the cooling liquid and shook his head.

Breakenridge glanced up at the sky. 'Moving out in ten minutes. Pick you up as we come through.'

'You better, man. Cos that ol' sun is murder on my complexion.'

Breakenridge laughed. 'Felix . . . before this trip's out, mebbe I'll let you ride up front with me.'

'Word is,' Tillman drawled, 'you honkies is gonna' be damn lucky to ever catch a ride in back with us.'

'Helluva world, ain't it? Ten minutes.' Suddenly both men stiffened, listening. Then they heard it plainly. The throbbing beat of a distant engine coming from the north. Instantly they sought cover at the base of the dune, searching the sky. It was Tillman who saw it first, identifying it with one explosive word.

'Chopper!'

Two miles away, sidelit by the rising sun, a whirring black insect was beating its way steadily towards them. A feeling of helplessness swept over Breakenridge. The one thing he had feared all along was the use of helicopters. With their great versatility they were capable of out-manoeuvring him at their leisure. He'd always known the possibility existed, but he'd hoped against hope that the vastness of the Sahara would give him the edge. That hope now seemed gone. In another minute or so it would be right over their position.

The thumping clatter of its rotor blades, combined with the whine of the twin turbines, rapidly increased in volume as the machine approached at about one thousand feet. Then he recognised it for what it was. He'd seen them in Vietnam, Mi-8 troop carriers. If it had a full load, there were twenty-eight fully-armed men up there. Add to them the ship's eight 57mm rockets and he and his men would be facing overwhelming fire-power.

The engine note changed as the machine suddenly began to lose height, descending rapidly towards the ground, a couple of hundred yards from where he crouched with Tillman. He watched until it disappeared behind the dunes and then heard the engine pitch rise as the pilot hovered. Moments later, the beat of the five rotor blades died away, the dunes acting as a series of natural baffles.

He tapped Tillman on the shoulder. 'Stay here. I'm gonna have a look-see.'

Crouching, he ran swiftly in the direction of the landed helicopter. As he drew closer he heard faint metallic sounds, carried on the still morning air. He dropped to the sand, wriggling forward on his elbows. Now he could hear the harsh guttural sounds of Arabic spoken. Then the helicopter in its drab sand-coloured camouflage was visible. The clam-shell side doors were open and soldiers were unloading weapons and equipment. Others had started digging weapon pits on either side of the *piste.* There was a leisurely air about their movements, typical of soldiers in every army on a boring, routine assignment. Clearly they were not expecting to go into immediate action. Two soldiers were even starting a small fire to brew up coffee.

Breakenridge studied the surrounding area, mind storing up information like a computer. When he was satisfied that he had gleaned all the information he needed, he withdrew, moving cautiously back the way he had come.

The others were clustered around the Mercedes, waiting for him.

'We got problems,' he said quietly. 'That chopper's a troop carrier, I counted mebbe twenty men. They're setting up a road block about three hundred yards up the track. They haven't seen us and don't expect us to be this close. That's the one thing we got working for us. Against us is the fact that the chopper c'n take off at any time to come looking. And if'n he does, he's gonna find us real quick. With those soldiers out there, we can't move. Five'll get you ten there's some of that bunch we hit yesterday coming up behind. That puts us between a rock an' a hard place."

'So what can we do?' Mathieu Talmont asked, running his fingers nervously through his grey hair.

'We hit that bunch up front an' we hit 'em hard. Before they get set.'

Breakenridge drew his combat knife and squatted down. They gathered around him in a circle as he began scoring a plan of the area in the sand with the blade.

'This is how we're gonna do it.'

Hale, Lachasse, Parker and Ramon struggled with the two Yamahas, heaving them bodily up the windward side of a long curving dune, cursing under their breath as they fought for purchase on the shifting slope. Reaching a point just below the skyline, they sank down, breathing heavily and sweating from the effort. After a few moments, Hale tapped his watch and held up his forefinger. One minute to go!

Willard crouched in Breakenridge's original observation point. Thirty yards away, the helicopter still squatted on the sand, its bulk between him and the soldiers at the road block, cutting them off from his view. Already he could feel the heat of the sun on the back of his neck. He glanced to his right.

Ten feet away sprawled Tillman and Bauer, the Negro cradling the five-and-a-half-pound projectile for the RPG-7 in his massive hands, the launcher ready in position on Bauer's shoulder. A movement at the corner of his eye caught his attention. He turned his head. The rotor blades on the helicoper were turning slowly. A puff of smoke came from the twin turbines as the engines burst into life. The mounting whine blasted at his eardrums as the blades became a whirling arc above the quivering machine. Frantically he signalled to Tillman.

In a flurry of movement the warhead was locked into position and Bauer stood up. Taking quick aim, he squeezed the trigger. An instant later the missile struck the port-side external fuel tank and the Mi-8 blew apart with a thunderous roar, sending cascades of liquid fire high into the air. Jagged bits of airframe cartwheeled outwards. A rotor blade scythed through two soldiers, severing legs from torsos. A blast of superheated air lifted Bauer off his feet and slammed him viciously against the ground. A remnant of the tail rotor hurtled end over end through the gap between Willard and Tillman, to bury itself in the sand beyond the stunned Bauer.

Groggily Willard staggered to his feet, fumbling with his AR-15, dimly aware of the screams of burning men. Then he heard the snarl of the Yamahas. They came catapulting off the top of the dune to land almost in the centre of the stupefied and dazed soldiers at the road block. Ramon and Lachasse sprayed them with raking bursts as Hale and Parker strove to keep the madly bucking machines upright. Then they were through, hammering away, gaining space to turn and come back for a second pass. Willard and Tillman opened up on the survivors, cutting them down like pins in a bowling alley. Finally, the bikes came in for the kill.

In all this carnage, and against the odds, one lone soldier kept his head and had sufficient coolness to hit back. Rolling into the machine-gun weapons pit, he grabbed the 7.62 PK, pulled the butt into his shoulder and fired a long steady burst at the leading Yamaha. Bullets ripped into the metal frame and engine, ricocheting upwards into Parker and Ramon. At full speed the bike veered off, then flipped end over end, its riders still aboard, like a macabre catherine wheel, into the burning remains of the helicopter.

As the bike's petrol tank blew with a dull 'whump', the Mercedes thundered into view along the track, Charroux hanging out of the passenger window firing his AR-15. Desperately, the machine-gunner tried to haul the awkward PK round to face the new threat, but he was too late.

Grim-faced, Breakenridge rode the thirty-six-ton juggernaut straight over him, pulping metal and flesh into an unrecognisable mush in the hot sand.

Pumping the brakes, he slewed the vehicle to a stop and jumped out, a .44 Magnum gripped in his fist. It was not needed. There were no survivors.

He slid the gun back in its holster and looked around him. The only sounds were the crackle of flames and the muted throb of the diesel. Willard and Tillman stumbled down the slope towards him, supporting Bauer between them. Slung over the black man's shoulder was the RPG-7. Hale jerked his Yamaha onto its stand, then moved in as close as he dared to the furnace heat of the burning wreckage, staring down at the funeral pyre of his friend.

Lachasse slapped a fresh magazine on his rifle, looked at Breakenridge and shrugged.

'Too bad, eh?'

Breakenridge nodded. 'Hale!'

The Englishman turned his head. 'What do you want?'

'Get on your bike and tell those civilians to get their asses up here on the double.'

Hale stared at him for a long moment. Wordlessly, he went to his bike, started it and rode away down the track. Behind him the fire licked greedily at the twisted remains of the other Yamaha.

Breakenridge went over to where Bauer was now sitting on the ground. The German appeared dazed.

'You get hit?'

Bauer shook his head. 'I got knocked out by the blast.'

'You better rest up for a while. Tillman, put him in the trailer. Sam!" Breakenridge jerked his head. Together, the two men walked to the Mercedes.

As they approached, Charroux pulled himself out from underneath it. 'No damage.' He grinned. 'Just blood.'

Reaching up into the cab, Breakenridge pulled out the map case and opened it. 'There's no way we can go any further on this track,' he told Sam. 'That chopper came in from the north. Which probably means that fort up there that we worried about is occupied.'

He lit a cigarette as Willard studied the map. It was a blow. They'd calculated on staying with the track for at least another hundred and fifty kilometres before turning west. Now that was out. They'd have to find another way.

'Pretty soon,' Breakenridge drawled, 'they're gonna be wondering where their fly boy's gotten to.'

'And come barrelling down here looking for him,' Willard finished.

'Uhuh!' Breakenridge nodded. 'So we better be long gone before they get here.'

Willard pointed to the map. 'There's a river bed marked there,' he said thoughtfully. 'Heads due west. Stops about forty kilometres short of the airstrip.'

His finger moved along a dotted line that meandered across the desert. It started about thirty kilometres from their present position. All they had to do was find it. He saw the look on the big man's face.

'If it's there,' Breakenridge said quietly. He closed the map case.

The Yamaha pulled to a stop a few yards away. He eyed the Englishman sitting astride the machine, remote, silent.

'I'll get Hale out looking for it.' The civilians, led by Guillard, came up the track to stand, shaken and silent, staring at the wreckage and the contorted bodies strewn around. Nose wrinkling at the stench of burnt flesh, Guillard stopped beside Breakenridge.

'You carve a bloody road, my friend.'

The slate-grey eyes bored into him. 'Would have gone around if'n I'd had the choice.'

Breakenridge became aware of the others and broke away from Guillard.

'What the hell are you people standing there for?' he demanded angrily. 'Mount up. On the double. Take off, Hale. We're rolling!'

CHAPTER FIFTEEN

On a scale of one to ten for optimism, their map registered a score of seven. The distance from the track to the start of the river bed had been nearer fifty kilometres than thirty, and over some of the roughest terrain they had yet encountered. Several times they'd come close to disaster. Once, the Mercedes had nearly overturned on a particularly bad section of going. The heat in the trailer had risen to almost that of a baker's oven. Just at the point where they had convinced themselves that the river bed was a figment of the cartographer's imagination, Hale had found it.

Like the furrow of a drunken giant's plough it zig-zagged through the grim landscape in a generally westward direction, bed cracked and eroded by sun and time. Guillard brought the Mercedes to a stop, the beat of its engine rough and irregular. Before he could switch off, it coughed and died on him. Within two minutes they had the cab tilted forward, exposing the V10 engine. Charroux carried out a brief inspection, then straightened up with a grimace.

'The filters are clogged with sand,' he announced.

'Can you fix it?' Breakenridge asked.

'Of course. I need petrol and a container of some kind. I will be as quick as I can.'

Breakenridge left him to it and walked forward along the river bed. He heard the high snarl of the Yamaha and stopped. Hale rode into view and pulled up beside him.

'What's it like up ahead?'

Hale took off his goggles and wiped a hand across cracked lips.

'I rode along it for about three miles,' he said hoarsely. 'There's a couple of places where sand's blown across. You'll have to watch that. It's two or three feet deep. I had trouble getting through the second one.'

Breakenridge uncorked his water bottle and gave it to him. Hale swilled his mouth out, spat and drank. He handed the bottle back.

'Wish you was a bleeding pub.' He accepted a cigarette. 'Reckon that plane'll be there?'

'We better hope so. Take a break. There's a problem with the engine. Soon as it's fixed we'll be on our way again.'

He went back to the truck. 'How's it going?' he asked Charroux. The Belgian waved an oily hand.

'If I had a franc for every time that question has been asked of me, I would not now be standing here.'

Breakenridge accepted the rebuke with a wry grin and walked on. He stopped beside Stephane who was standing in the meagre shade offered by the side of the trailer.

'How's things in back?' He kept his voice neutral, aware that every word spoken could be heard by others.

She shrugged tiredly. 'We're alive. We will manage.'

'Just hang in there. With luck we'll be out of this stinking country by late tomorrow.'

He saw her eyes widen questioningly and turned away, avoiding her obvious query.

Slowly the air temperature built up, until at midday it stood at one hundred degrees Fahrenheit, turning the wadi into a cauldron, the merciless heat sucking oxygen from the atmosphere. They were pinned to the sand beneath the trailer, each one locked into a private hell where movement only increased their suffering. Salt tablets were passed out to combat dehydration, grease smeared on cracked lips. Imprisoned, they could only wait.

The one affected most was Charroux. Even though a canvas awning had been erected to shade him from the worst effects of the sun, he could only work for a few minutes at a time. Insidiously, in spite of the salt tablets and continual drinking of water, dehydration ate away at him, affecting his judgement. Doggedly he forced himself to concentrate, knowing that everything depended upon his skill. Without the truck they were dead.

At two o'clock he pressed the starter. The diesel coughed into life, ran for a few moment, then died. Juggling with the priming, he tried again. This time it roared healthily. He stood, wiping his hands on a piece of rag, listening to the steady beat. He looked up as Breakenridge and Willard appeared beside him.

'She works again.' He grinned tiredly and blipped the throttle. 'We can move.'

'Roust 'em out, Sam. We been here too long.' Breakenridge reached up and ripped down the awning from over the engine. Charroux leaned across and operated the hydraulic pump to bring the cab back into position. Smoothly it tilted through seventy degrees.

Lethargically, people began moving out from beneath the trailer in response to Willard's urgent commands, trying to shake off a collective torpor.

Breakenridge put a hand on Charroux's arm. 'You've done good today. When we—'

A red flower blossomed suddenly in the centre of Charroux's forehead and he slammed back against the side of the cab. A split second later the flat whip-crack of a rifle-shot echoed across the wadi.

As Charroux's body toppled to the ground, Breakenridge was spinning away and down, clawing for the Magnum on his hip. A second bullet shattered the side window of the cab. Another gouged a ragged hole in the trailer. People scattered in shocked surprise, diving for cover. Gripping the Magnum two-handed, he desperately searched for the source of the attack.

A ricochet whined off the trailer chassis, screaming past his ear. Then he saw it: a muzzle flash from the crest of a dune.

'Two o'clock high,' he yelled above the sound of the still-running diesel. An AR-15 opened up. Then the rest of the team swelled the chorus, saturating the dune's high ridge with flying lead, creating a miniature sandstorm that marched along its entire length.

The incoming fire stopped. Whoever it was was either dead or keeping his head well down.

'Mount up,' Breakenridge bellowed. He squeezed the trigger until the .44 was empty, then dived for the cab, wrenching the door open and throwing himself up into the seat, grabbing for the controls. The rest of the team bundled the civilians into the trailer and kept up an intermittent fire, covering each other as one by one they climbed aboard the already moving Mercedes. Hale gunned the Yamaha away down the wadi as Guillard hauled himself up into the cab alongside Breakenridge.

'Where the hell did they come from?' he shouted over the din of gunfire and the engine.

'If'n you're that fuckin' curious, go back an' ask 'em.'

Breakenridge heaved on the wheel to avoid a deep crack in the wadi bed. At that instant the big mirror outboard of his door disintegrated under the impact of a high-velocity bullet, spraying shards of glass and metal into the cab. A fragment sliced across his left cheek. Involuntarily he ducked his head aside and for a moment lost control of the Mercedes. It slewed to one side, scraping its entire length against the bank of the wadi.

Panelling crumpled under the impact as the heavy vehicle ploughed forward. Then it veered outward from the bank and Breakenridge managed to regain control, guiding his unwieldy charge around a sharp bend and out of the line of incoming fire.

On top of the dune behind them, the captain got to his feet and rammed home a fresh magazine on the AK-47. Below him, the crumpled body of Charroux lay sprawled in the sand. He felt a slight glow of satisfaction. He'd managed to turn the tables at last. He'd seen the big man go down. With luck, he'd wounded him. Now they were trapped, forced to stay in the wadi for its entire length. All he had to do was follow and pick them off.

He turned and waved up the lumbering ZIL, pointing to the wadi, effectively corking the bottle, preventing the Mercedes from doubling back. When he had first encountered the stopped vehicle, it had been a surprise to him. He had not expected to come upon them so soon or to be in a position of tactical advantage when he did so. The noise of his jeep crossing the dunes in low gear had been blanketed by the sound of the heavy diesel. Unfortunately he had not been able to wait for the rest of his men to arrived in the ZIL and had been forced to attack at once.

Another surprise had been the small number of men pitted against him. After his own bloody setbacks, and having discovered the debacle with the helicopter, he'd expected to be confronted by at least twenty. The inescapable conclusion forced upon him was either that these men were exceptionally good or his own troops were exceedingly bad. He decided that from now on circumspection would be his best ally. Take a leaf from their book. Hit and pull back.

Tillman and Bauer crouched behind a drift of sand, blown into the wadi by the harsh summer *sirocco,* the sweat evaporating almost instantly on their bodies, leaving behind a thin salty film on the flesh. Faintly they could hear the oncoming ZIL, the engine muted by the high banks of the twisting river bed. As the sound grew louder, Tillman locked home the rocket on the RPG-7. He grinned.

Bauer studied him for a moment. Then he said: 'Something amuses you?'

The big Negro chuckled softly. 'Was jes' thinking, man. How's about you'n me going into business?'

'Business?'

'Yeah! We'd make a great team. Black an' White Wreckers Inc.'

Bauer appeared to consider the idea. He nodded. 'Perhaps now is a good time to start.'

The sound of the ZIL was now very close, just around the bend ahead of them, fifty yards away. Bauer tightened his grip on the launcher. Twenty seconds later the round slatted nose of the approaching vehicle came into view. He picked his aiming point – the divided windshield. The truck was now head on, bearing down on him. He waited until the last possible moment. When the truck's windshield filled the optical sight he squeezed the trigger. At the same instant the launcher was smashed violently sideways into his face. He felt himself falling, saw the ground coming up to meet him.

The warhead screamed off at a tangent and blew a hole in the wadi bank some ten feet ahead of the advancing truck. Tillman saw the truck veer away and strike the opposite bank. It reared up as though trying to climb the steeply shelving side, then overturned, spilling men out of the back as it crashed to the wadi floor.

The AR-15 bucked as he fired an extended burst high and to his right, searching out the marksman who had shot the launcher out of Bauer's hands. Earth kicked up around him as fire came in from another direction. Desperately, he threw himself sideways, landing alongside Bauer behind the shallow protection of the sandbar. Bullets whanged into the banking above his head.

As he rammed home a fresh magazine, Bauer groaned and stirred. Tillman slapped a massive hand on his back, holding him down.

'Hold it, man. We're in trouble.'

Cautiously, he tried changing his position to get a view of the soldiers from the truck, but only succeeded in drawing further fire. He realised now that he and Bauer were trapped. It was only a matter of time before the Algerians pulled themselves together and came swarming all over them.

'Shee-it!' he said softly.

He glanced down at Bauer. The right side of the German's face was laid open from jaw to cheekbone by the impact of the launcher. Blood flowed from a vicious-looking cut across the bridge of his nose where the optical sight had caught it. He didn't look to be in any condition to fight.

Now Tillman could hear movement and voices from his front. The soldiers from the truck were obviously under command again, being readied for an attack. He took a grenade from his pocket and hooked a thumb through the loop of the pin. Before he could pull and throw, someone opened up from behind him. He recognised the distinctive sound of an AR-15. Then another joined in, the rounds whispering low over his head. Screams came from the wadi. There was more firing, some of it ragged, coming from the Algerians.

The AR-15 laid in burst after burst. He heard Breakenridge's bellow above the din.

'Tillman! . . . Bauer! . . . Get your asses outta there. NOW!'

Tillman drew the pin, lobbed the grenade and grabbed hold of Bauer. Hoisting the semi-conscious man across his back, he wriggled along the wadi. Suddenly Breakenridge was there.

'Come on . . . move!'

Taking an arm each, they half dragged, half carried Bauer towards the waiting Mercedes. Just as they reached it, there was a prolonged burst of heavy firing behind them. Willard ran into view, stopped, turned and dropped to one knee, AR-15 levelled. Lachasse appeared, moving fast, weaving from side to side as he ran.

Willard opened up as soon as the Corsican was past him, raking the length of the wadi to his front. Breakenridge hauled the panting Lachasse up into the trailer.

'Sam!'

At Breakenridge's shout, Willard got to his feet and ran towards the already moving Mercedes. He caught up with it, tossed his rifle up to Lachesse and threw himself aboard. As he lay on the floor, chest heaving, he heard Breakenridge open up above his head.

Hauling himself upright, he looked back through the open doorway. High up, speeding along the top of a dune parallel to the wadi was a jeep. He nudged Breakenridge and pointed. The big American swung his AR-15 in its direction and emptied the magazine. A line of bullets kick up sand in the jeep's path and it slewed to a halt, the occupants throwing themselves out. Then it was gone, hidden from sight by an intervening dune.

Dieter Bauer sat on the bunk, teeth clenched, eyes closed as Stephane wound new bandaging around his wounded face and head. There was a whimpering sound from the next bunk and she glanced across to see Marie-Claire stirring restlessly in drugged sleep.

Breakenridge came into the trailer, moving quietly on rubber-soled boots. He stopped beside the German. 'How're you feeling?'

Bauer opened his eyes. 'Better,' he said stiffly. 'With such a pretty nurse, how could I not?'

Breakenridge grinned at Stephane. 'You ever want to take this up permanent I c'n guarantee a steady supply of customers.'

She shuddered. 'I think not.'

He moved past her to the auxiliary fuel tank at the front of the trailer. Unscrewing the filler cap, he slid in a dipstick. Withdrawing it, he inspected the level in the dim glow of the roof light. It was being used up with alarming speed, the result of constant low gear work. With luck, it should last for the remaining forty or so kilometres to the airstrip. If Tuck failed to make the rendezvous, then it wouldn't matter a damn. Because that was the end of the line.

'Is something wrong?' Stephane's voice broke into his thoughts. He turned. Bauer had gone. He held out the dipstick.

'Fuel's getting low.'

She touched the length of plaster on his left cheek. 'It needs changing.'

He replaced the filler cap, went to the bunk vacated by Bauer and sat down wearily. 'My Medicaid payments are long overdue.'

She stared at him uncomprehendingly.

'Sorry,' he said quietly. 'I guess I say things like that most of the time.' He pointed to his face. 'You want to fix this?'

She nodded and got to work. After a few moments she said: 'You're a strange man.'

'Yeah?'

There was a guarded look in his eyes. Stephane dabbed at the wound on his cheek with a pad soaked in antiseptic and saw him wince.

'Sometimes you give the impression you hate the whole world. Then, at other times, you are so different, more human, not so frightening.'

He said nothing, grey eyes studying her in the poor light. She felt uncomfortable under the steady gaze and looked away, busying herself with the fresh dressing.

'You did not volunteer for this duty.' She avoided his eyes as she taped the dressing in place on his cheek. 'There, it is finished.'

His hand closed on her wrist, firmly but gently. 'How did you know that?'

'Guillard.'

'What about him?' His voice was hard.

'The conversation you had with him that morning. I have thought about it. He has some kind of hold over you, doesn't he?'

Breakenridge released her wrist, took out a pack of Disque Bleu and offered one to her. After he had lit their cigarettes, he said: 'It matter that much to you?' There was a flat don't-give-a-damn note in his voice.

She drew in smoke, expelling it slowly. 'I think so,' she said, low voiced.

He looked towards the open end of the trailer, staring out at the night sky framed in the doorway.

'They laid an argument on me I couldn't win.'

'They?'

'Guillard. And the men he works for.'

She stared at him. 'Men? What men?'

He sighed. 'Your own security services.'

'Oh.'

'That's about the size of it.' He stood up to face her. 'No more questions. No more answers.'

She was very close to him. 'He is not to be trusted,' she said softly. 'He has much—' she searched for the word '—animosity towards you. Take care.'

He looked down at her, his eyes softening a fraction.

'Buy you a drink sometime.'

After he'd gone, she sat staring into space, her mind a kaleidoscope of thoughts, trying to see the possibility of a future beyond the next few hours.

A sudden sound jerked her back to the reality of the present. She looked up. Tillman was standing beside the other bunk, looking down at the sleeping form of Marie-Claire.

'She's still the same.' Stephane stood up. 'No change.'

Tillman didn't look up. 'She ever gonna get any better?'

Stephane pulled the oversize parka closer around her body, fighting back her tiredness. There was a strange pleading quality underlying the big Negro's question.

'Perhaps.'

He shook his head slowly, baffled by a situation that was beyond him.

'It ain't right,' he said angrily. His huge fists balled. 'It jes' ain't right.'

He turned away abruptly and moved to the open doorway. For an instant, his huge frame blotted out the stars.

'G'night ma'am.'

Then he was gone.

CHAPTER SIXTEEN

One hour before sun-up the Mercedes set out on the final leg of its journey. Breakenridge was fully aware of the dangers involved in travelling over this kind of terrain in the dark, but he decided that really he had no choice. They'd killed only a few of those soldiers yesterday, and the rest would be coming after them. To wait until dawn before moving would be to invite an attack. The airstrip was forty kilometres away. If he could reach it before the Algerians could guess his destination, it would buy them much-needed time to make a home run in the Dakota.

Through the windshield he could see the tail-light of the Yamaha glowing red in the darkness as it broke trail for him. Somewhere ahead should be another *piste*. It was up to Hale to find it.

The river bed gradually gave way to high dunes, then finally petered out. He felt the drag of soft sand on the wheels and sent up a silent prayer that they wouldn't bog down at this stage. Without warning, the motion was different. They were running free on the rough surface of the *piste*. Thus far his luck had held.

He spared a brief glance for the man sitting alongside him.

'Well, how's it feel?'

'Like the ride, man. But hate the view.'

Breakenridge grinned. 'Trouble with you second-class citizens, you ain't never satisfied.'

Tillman's face creased into a broad smile. 'Hey, don't knock it. Us professional underdogs has only got one way to go, baby. An' that's up!'

'Welcome to the tax-payin' classes, brother.'

Tillman grimaced. 'Ouch!'

Breakenridge dropped the banter and concentrated on the ground ahead. It had been a long time since anyone had used this track. In places, wind-drifted sand bars showed up in the headlights, forcing him to drop down into crawler gear, inching the huge vehicle forward. Several times Hale came back to warn of impossible sections ahead. Then followed the time-consuming business of discovering a way round the obstacle before they could make further progress.

Imperceptibly the sky began to lighten to the east. Their other enemy, dawn, was reaching out for them, bringing with it the threat of discovery. The constant strain of manhandling the thirty-six tonner over the almost impossible going was beginning to tell on Breakenridge. Sharp twinges of pain lanced through his shoulder and neck muscles. His eyes grew red-rimmed and gritty from the unrelenting concentration. The only satisfaction came from seeing the kilometres ticking up on the trip meter. It had been set at zero before they moved off. When it registered twenty-five it would be time to turn west for the airstrip. He glanced down. Twenty-four point eight.

It was now light enough to see without aid from the headlights. He switched them off and stared through the windshield, searching for a suitable piece of ground to make the turn. He saw Hale signal and swing left between two high dunes. Changing down, he prepared to negotiate the turn. The sand looked firm enough to stand the weight of the Mercedes. As he got closer, he powered up the engine and began feeding the rim of the wheel through his hands, aiming for the point where Hale had ridden between the two dunes.

The first bullet starred the windshield, passed between Breakenridge and Tillman, and buried itself somewhere in the rear of the cab. The second took off the nearside wiper arm; the third gouged a long furrow in the metal roof of the cab and struck the trailer.

Breakenridge ducked, jerking the wheel to the left. The instrument panel exploded into fragments of metal and glass. He heard Tillman shout, 'Look out!'

Before he could regain control, the Mercedes punched its blunt nose into the base of a dune, the impact hurling both men forward against the restraining straps of their safety belts. Momentarily dazed and shaken, they remained sprawled in their seats. Then Breakenridge recovered and released his seat harness. He stayed hunched down, aware that the firing had stopped. His eyes met Tillman's.

'It came in from high right,' he said. 'We'll go out my door. Keep the truck between them and us. You ready?'

Tillman nodded. Breakenridge reached over and eased off the door catch. He pushed. The door stayed shut. Obviously something was jamming it. He squirmed around and brought both knees up to his chin. Then he aimed a violent double-footed kick at the door panel. It swung out under the blow with a screech of tortured metal and stopped, half open.

They went out through the opening fast and low, AR-15s clutched in their hands, then crouched back to back between the side of the trailer and the shelter of the dune. Still no one fired. Whoever had ambushed them was waiting, biding his time until a target presented itself.

'That,' whispered Tillman over his shoulder, 'is positively the first an' last time I take a ride up front with a white brother. They always got somethin' sneaky goin' on.'

'Well, let that be a lesson to you, darkie,' Breakenridge threw back.

They tensed at the heavy report of a Smith & Wesson, its typical 'boom' reverberating among the dunes on the other side of the truck.

'Hale,' Breakenridge said flatly.

There was an answering burst of fire from AK-47s, like ripping calico. The Smith & Wesson boomed twice more, followed closely by the faint snarl of the Yamaha.

'That ol' boy's gonna need some help.'

Breakenridge nodded and banged with his clenched fist on the side of the trailer.

'Sam!'

'Yo.' Willard's muffled voice answered him.

'Get set to come out fast. Everyone. Wait for my word.'

He glanced over his shoulder at Tillman. 'Felix. Get down under the trailer. Pick off anyone who shows.'

Tillman dropped down in the sand and wriggled his bulk under the chassis to a position beneath the spare wheel and alongside the first of the trailer wheels. From here he had a good view of the ground in front of and above him.

'Set,' he called in a low voice.

Once again the sound of the Yamaha rose on the still morning air, this time much closer. There was a renewed burst of firing.

The butt of Breakenridge's rifle thudded against the trailer. 'Go!'

Beneath the trailer, Tillman heard the doors crash open. High above him on the crest of a dune, he saw movement and took aim. Before he could squeeze the trigger, Hale skittered into view from behind a low dune to his right and came flat-out, crouched forward over the handlebars towards the Mercedes, arrow-straight across the open ground.

The head and shoulders of a man showed on the skyline of the dune, automatic rifle swinging round to take a bead on the flying Englishman. Tillman's teeth showed in a savage grin as he squeezed the trigger of the AR-15. The man atop the dune seemed to hesitate. Then he was falling, rifle dropping from his hands, tumbling out and down, to finish sprawled and still, half-way up the steep slope.

Breakenridge came to his feet, moving fast to the back of the trailer as the occupants scrambled out. Guillard jumped down, diving for cover in the shelter of the trailer. Breakenridge grabbed him. 'Get the civilians under cover away from here. Stay with 'em. They may have to fight.'

As he shouldered past, he noted that each one was armed. If the time came, he hoped to Christ they knew which end was which. At that moment Hale skidded to a stop in front of him.

'The bastards let me go by, then jumped you.'

'How many?'

'I counted six. And a jeep. Over there.' Hale pointed over his shoulder. 'In the dunes. Army.'

Breakenridge glanced at Willard. 'Sam. Try to take the high ground. I'm going with Hale.' He swung astride the pillion.

The Englishman looked at him questioningly.

'Try an' get in behind 'em. See if'n we can't dust their asses.'

Hale nodded, slipped the machine into gear and they were away, out into the open and tearing for the dunes. Breakenridge slitted his eyes against the wind whipping into his face and hung on as the Yamaha bucked and kicked under him. The snarling howl of the engine filled his ears. A strange exhilaration compounded of speed and danger built up within him. Gouts of sand sprang up in a broken line to his left, matching their wild pace. They were under fire.

'Incoming!' he yelled at the top of his voice. He saw Hale's head jerk in quick acknowledgement.

'Hang on!'

The bike leant over at a seemingly impossible angle, footrests almost scraping the ground as Hale curved it away to the right. Then they were among the dunes, soft sand dragging at the wheels, slowing them.

Hale let go of his left handlebar grip for a fraction, pointing up, so that the Yamaha was swinging left, climbing like a frightened cat up the steep flank of a dune. Breakenridge saw the crest rushing towards them and the bowl of the pearly grey morning sky beyond. It was as though they were about to leap off the end of the world. At once the bike seemed to kick hard right, and they were running along the ridge.

Below, in a valley among the dunes they saw a jeep, two men running towards it. Breakenridge fired a quick burst in their direction from his AR-15. They threw themselves flat. Before he could fire again, the Yamaha was off the crest and bucketing back down the way they had come.

Without warning, the front wheel dug into deep soft sand. The machine jack-knifed, catapulting the two men outwards. Breakenridge saw the ground rushing up to meet him and instinctively curled into a ball before hitting. He felt the impact jar his entire body. Then he was rolling and sliding in a wild flurry of sand before jolting to a stop. Before he had a chance to collect himself, Hale cannoned into him. The impact knocked the breath out of both of them.

They lay, gasping. Then Breakenridge sat up, clawing sand from his face. The ominous sound of heavy gunfire penetrated his mind. It was coming from the direction of the Mercedes, AK-47s intermingled with AR-15s.

Hale got to his feet, swaying, and started up the slope to where the machine lay. Breakenridge went to help him pull it upright. Hale gave the Yamaha a cursory check, and tried the starter. It fired at once. Breakenridge retrieved his rifle, wiped it clean of sand, then swung on behind Hale.

'Circle around an' try to come in where we saw that jeep.'

Hale gunned the engine, let it run for a few moments, slipped it into gear, and cautiously picked a way down to level ground. The jeep and the two men were gone by the time they got there, and the firing was now intermittent, short bursts mixed with single shots. Breakenridge stared down the valley, his eyes following the fresh tyre tracks in the sand. He pointed off to the left.

'Make for the top of that dune. Mebbe we can see where they're at.'

Hale unscrewed the filler cap on the tank and peered in.

'We're nearly out of petrol,' he warned.

Breakenridge gave him a bleak look. 'So's the rest of the fuckin' world.' He settled himself on the pillion. 'Get moving.'

Ten feet below the skyline, Hale pulled the machine sideways and switched off. They went the rest of the way on their bellies. Breakenridge eased forward the last few inches and peered over.

Below, like a broken and discarded toy, stood the Mercedes. He could see no sign of movement. All firing had stopped. An oppressive silence hung over the place. For all he could tell, everyone down there was dead. A brief thought of Stephane came into his mind. He brushed it aside, concentrating on trying to spot the enemy. Wherever they were, they were well hidden.

From somewhere away to the right, the sound of an engine broke the silence. He tapped Hale on the shoulder and pointed north. They slid back down below the crest, got to their feet and ran towards the source of the noise.

The dune curved back on itself in a wide semi-circle, with the crest rising high in front of them. Panting, they hauled themselves to the top. Below and to their left, about two hundred yards away, was the jeep. Two men sat in it, waiting as three others ran towards it.

Breakenridge flopped down, tucked the butt of the AR-15 into his shoulder, selected single shot and lined up on the man in the driving seat. He fired. The man jerked round in surprise, then waved an arm at the three running men. The jeep began to move. Cursing silently, Breakenridge shifted his aim and fired at the rear tyre. Sand spurted just short of the target.

One of the men on foot loosed off a wild burst in his direction.

He ducked as bullets hummed around the top of the dune. When he raised his head again, the last man was flinging himself on board and the jeep was accelerating away. He lifted the AR-15 to fire, then changed his mind. The Algerians were on the run, and there was no point in wasting ammunition.

Wearily he got to his feet. Glancing at his watch, he realised with a shock that a full hour had passed since the start of the attack. They'd have to get under way as soon as possible.

As they trudged back to the bike, Hale said: 'They'll be back.'

Breakenridge nodded. There wasn't a damn thing he could do about it. They got on the bike and headed for the Mercedes.

As it came into view he could see figures moving about. The roar of the wind in his ears and the snarl of the Yamaha engine obliterated the sound of the heavy diesel, but he could see the vehicle juddering violently and inching back from the base of the dune, flinging up fountains of sand from the drive wheels as it slowly freed itself.

He jumped off the bike almost before it had stopped. Willard hurried towards him.

'Any casualties?' he shouted above the bellowing of the engine.

'One!'

He saw the look on Willard's face. 'Who?'

'Marie-Claire. She's dead.'

At that moment the diesel coughed, picked up, spluttered and then died. He swung away from Willard and ran to the cab. The starter whirred again and again.

'What th' hell's wrong?'

Guillard glared down at him through the shattered windshield.

'How should I know? It just cut out.'

'Well, keep trying fercrissakes!'

'Naturally.' Guillard's voice was heavy with sarcasm. 'Did you think I was going to get out and sunbathe?'

The starter whirred again, grinding at the engine. Barely able to contain his impatience, Breakenridge turned away.

Willard put a hand on his arm. 'I think you'd better come and look at the girl.'

'Not now, Sam.' He pulled free.

'It's important.'

Breakenridge sighed. 'It had better be.'

He followed Willard to the back of the trailer, passing Matis, de Payeux and Talmont. A few feet further on, Jean-Paul stood beside Stephane. No one spoke, but he felt their eyes watching him as he climbed up into the trailer. Inside, it was hot and fetid. Equipment and belongings littered the floor, knocked over in the rush to get out. Daylight filtered in through bullet holes in the sides. At the far end, Tillman stood silently beside one of the lower bunks on which lay the blanket-covered form of Marie-Clair. Flies buzzed eagerly around the bloodstain on the blanket and the blood seeping from below the bunk.

'She's dead, man.'

Breakenridge was surprised at the flat anger in Tillman's voice. He knew the big Negro had become strangely attached to the girl over the past few days and he would have expected some kind of reaction, but not the unconcealed ferocity that glared at him from the other's eyes.

'Easy on there, Felix,' he said gently. 'None of us wanted this to happen.'

Tillman reached down, grabbed the blanket and jerked it back. 'Well you jes' take a closer look, man. 'Cos sure as shit, somebody did!'

Breakenridge looked at him, then down at the body. Marie-Claire lay flat on her back, eyes wide open in a final expression of surprise, the expression that Breakenridge had seen so many times in people's faces when death had come for them unexpectedly.

His eyes moved on down to the wound. The bullet had entered the left breast and torn through the heart. It seemed simple enough at a glance, but he sensed that something was wrong. Vaguely he heard the starter grinding round. It stopped. He looked away at the uneven line of bullet holes in the side of the trailer. Marie-Claire must have been on her feet when she was hit.

'No way.' Willard spoke as if knowing what was in his mind. 'Look at the floor beneath the bunk.'

Breakenridge crouched down. There, directly below the body of the dead girl, was a bullet hole. By the size of it, a heavy calibre. His fingers explored the underside of the bunk. There was a hole in the canvas. Slowly he stood up. Tillman and Willard waited silently. He raised his eyes, searching the roof. There were no entry holes.

He straightened the blanket. Now he could see the powder burns and scorch marks in the rough wool.

'Murder,' he said softly. Willard nodded. Tillman closed the girl's staring eyes and slid the blanket over her face.

'Why?' Tillman said harshly. 'Why kill her? She wasn't doin' no harm.'

'How come she was in here?' Breakenridge asked.

'We had to get out in a hurry.' Willard shook his head. 'I guess we just forgot all about her.' Breakenridge stared round the trailer. The killing didn't make sense. Someone had come back in here during the attack and had deliberately shot the girl. What the hell for? She was half out of her mind, drugged most of the time and no obvious threat to anyone. Unless . . .

Then he saw it. The thing that had been staring him in the face all the time. The reason for the girl's death. He pushed past Tillman and picked up an empty five-gallon petrol can.

'Here's the reason.' He held it out. They stared at it, then back to him. 'Someone got desperate. So they took an almighty chance. Snuck back in here during the attack, dumped a full can of gasoline in the diesel tank. The girl must have come round an' seen whoever it was. They couldn't take a chance she wouldn't say anything, so they shot her.'

'How can you be so sure?'

'Whoever it was,' Breakenridge said grimly, 'made one small mistake. They forgot to replace the filler cap on the tank. I screwed it down good and tight last night after I dipped it.'

He pointed to the floor beside the tank. The filler cap lay there. Tillman went to the tank, bent over the filler hole and sniffed. He straightened up and turned.

'Gasoline.'

'Which is why,' Breakenridge said, 'this truck has reached the end of the line. From here on in, we walk. Felix, go tell Guillard to stop wasting his time.'

As the big Negro moved past him, he said: 'What about the bastard that killed her?'

'I'll find him.'

'Make sure I'm around when you do, man.'

After he'd gone, Willard said: 'Any ideas on who it is?'

'A couple. But I want to be good an' sure, Sam. Because whoever it is ain't gonna get to use his return ticket.'

While Willard began getting everyone together for the march to the airstrip, Breakenridge climbed up into the cab for the last time and reached down under the lower bunk, groping for the handle of the canvas grip which contained the portable two-way radio transmitter he'd stowed there before leaving Marseilles. As he pulled it clear, he saw that someone else had beaten him to it.

A heavy calibre bullet had smashed the radio beyond repair. The odds were that it had come from the same gun that had killed Marie-Claire. And whoever had pulled the trigger had likely killed the rest of them by his action. There was now no way he could contact Don Tuck and call him in for the pick-up.

A wave of black despair and fury swept over him. His fist smashed down on the back of the seat. All that goddamned effort for nothing. Gradually his self-control reasserted itself and he forced himself to think, as coldly and dispassionately as possible. Finally, he knew there was just one faint, one negligible chance. If it came off, they'd live. If not . . .

He jumped down. The others stood there waiting, each loaded with water, ammunition and weapons. His eyes flicked over them, studying faces. One of those faces hid a killer. Tillman appeared from behind the trailer and threw a spade on the sand.

'I buried her,' he said bleakly. Hale started the Yamaha and throttled the engine back. Breakenridge slung the AR-15 on his shoulder and stepped forward.

'I got somethin' to say to all of you. Only gonna say it one time. So you listen an' you listen good.'

He paused. Nobody moved. The silence grew uncomfortable. When he was positive he held their complete attention, he went on:

'I intend making a forced march. Now some of you know what that means. But those of you that don't are sure as hell gonna find out. The hard way!'

Again he paused. The faces of his men were devoid of all expression. They knew what he had in mind for them, and it would be far from pleasant.

He concentrated on the civilians. 'We got fifteen kilometres to go. Mebbe you people don't think that sounds far. Well I'm here to tell you it's gonna feel more like a hundred an' fifteen by the time we get to where we're going.'

He jerked his thumb over his shoulder. 'Out there the sun'll scramble your brain an' the sand'll fry your feet. After you walked a hundred yards you'll want to rest up. The hell you will! If'n I got to kick your goddamn asses ever' inch of the fuckin' way, you'll keep moving on. One step at a time. Left foot in front of th' right. Nobody drops out. Less'n of course you're dead. Even then, you don't do it 'less I say so. Likewise you only drink when I tell you. You all got weapons. More'n likely, we'll get jumped. Then you're gonna have to use 'em to keep alive. Jes' one more thing. Anyone don't like my style, well fuck you an' th' horse you rode up on!'

He noticed Tillman shaking his head from side to side.

'Tillman! Take point. Hale! Right flank. Guillard! Stick with the civilians. Sam! Take Bauer an' Lachasse. You got th' rearguard.'

The commands were rapped out, hard and fast, like single-spaced shots. Breakenridge swung round to face west.

'Move off!'

Tillman padded past. Twenty paces behind came the civilians with Guillard. Before the rearguard reached him, Breakenridge took up station on the left flank.

As they reached the dunes, he spared a look back. The Mercedes sat there, broken, forlorn, like a wounded animal waiting to be put down. Somewhere close by was an unmarked grave.

CHAPTER SEVENTEEN

The captain lit a cigarette and spun the spent match out through the open doors of the trailer. The murmur of voices drifted up to him from outside. He glanced at his watch again. It was over two hours since he'd sent the jeep back for the remainder of his men, and he was impatient for its return. As soon as it arrived he could take up the pursuit again. Now everything was in his favour. The enemy were reduced to walking, the presence of the civilians obviously slowing them down. He had transport, he outnumbered them, and he knew their direction of march. Tactically he was in a superior position, able to dictate where and how he would fight.

Only one thing puzzled him. From the abandoned Mercedes the tracks led westward. One of his men had followed them for some distance and there had been no deviation in their course. It was now impossible for him accept that they were making for the Moroccan border, as that lay some four hundred kilometres distant. So where were they going?

He stared down at the map spread across his knees. There was only one place for hundreds of kilometres where they could be going: the airstrip. But that didn't make sense. It had been in use as an emergency landing place ever since the French had left the Sahara. Surely they wouldn't stake everything on the slim chance of stealing an aircraft. Yet it seemed the only logical explanation to fit the facts. The big man had done the unexpected before. Why not again?

On the other hand, their every movement so far bore the mark of having been planned, down to the finest detail. Why, then, leave the last and most vital section unplanned? Or had they?

Frustration built up in him as his mind went round and round the problem. Somewhere, just beyond his reach, lay the answer. He scrubbed a hand tiredly across his face, wincing at the pain from his broken ribs as he did so. There was only one thing he could do and that was to work on the assumption that the airstrip was their target, and head for it in the jeep with the majority of his men. The others would have to follow the tracks on foot and cut off any retreat.

A shout from outside distracted him. He looked through the doorway. The lookout on the dune was waving. The jeep had arrived with reinforcements.

'Take a mouthful, swill it around, an' spit it out. Then drink easy. Don't gulp.'

Breakenridge's hoarse croak penetrated numbed minds, forcing sluggish limbs into fumbling movement. He watched the five ex-hostages stand swaying in their tracks like used-up pack mules, every vestige of expression wiped clean from their faces by the three hours of purgatory they'd endured in that cauldron of blazing sun and red-hot sand. Cracked lips and swollen tongues sucked gratefully at lukewarm water. Mathieu Talmont bowed his grey head and sank to his knees.

Breakenridge stepped in, grabbed him by the front of his shirt and hauled him upright again. The glazed eyes stared vacantly into his.

'You,' Breakenridge snarled. 'Stay on your goddamned feet.'

Jean-Paul lurched forward to support the older man. A finger jabbed painfully into his chest.

'Get your ass back into line, sonny. Heroics is for fifty cent novels.'

Rebellion flared briefly on the young man's sun-flayed face. Then it was gone, and he fell back into line. Breakenridge looked away to the distant figure of Tillman standing patiently waiting out in front. He waved an arm. The Negro turned and plodded forward. One by one, the group swayed and jerked into motion like a broken-backed snake.

Breakenridge dropped back and fell in beside Stephane as she struggled doggedly through the yielding sand, the rifle on her shoulder weighing her down.

'Gonna ask you some questions. Jes' concentrate on puttin' one foot in front of th' other. Answer me in your own time. All right?'

She nodded, not looking at him, her eyes fixed on the ground a few feet ahead.

'Take your mind back to the fort. Just before we hit it, one of your people was out of the room. Think about it. Take your time. I want the name.'

She kept walking, not answering him.

'You told me that when you tried to escape, they were waiting for you. What did you mean?'

She looked up at him, eyes enormous in her drawn face. She staggered and he caught her before she fell. Recovering, she moved on, a step at a time.

'It was night.' Her voice was just above a whisper. She paused. Left foot. Right foot. Left foot. 'We opened the door. They were waiting just outside.' Breath rasped in her throat.

'Like they knew.'

He made the words a statement, not a question. She gave no sign that she'd heard. Glancing ahead, he saw that they'd dropped back a few paces, lagging behind the others.

'Stephane.' He took hold of her arm. 'I know you want to close it off, but there's some things I need to know. Now!'

His fingers tightened. With an effort she lifted her head, staring at the bowed backs in front.

'What?' she said dully.

'How many of you people use cigarettes?'

The question was so unexpected that she floundered to a halt. He pushed her on.

'Keep goin', damn you!' His voice bit into her harshly.

She stumbled forward, remembering the lesson. Left. Right. Left. Right.

'The answer. Come on.'

The relentless drive of the man hammered at her, forcing her to think.

'Jean-Paul.' Pause. 'Matis.'

'And you.'

She nodded.

'That all?'

'Yes!' She wanted to scream the word at him but all that came out was a croak.

Across to his right he saw the motionless figure of Hale astride his bike, stopped at the top of a low dune, binoculars raised to his eyes.

He shifted his gaze back to Stephane. 'So which one was out of the room the night we hit the fort?'

After a moment her lips formed a word.

He bent closer. 'Say that again.'

The name was a whisper, nearly drowned in the noise of the fast-approaching Yamaha. Breakenridge let go of her, leaving her to stumble on as he cut away to meet Hale.

'Dust cloud.' He saw the muscles in the Englishman's throat contract painfully as he tried to get the words out. 'North. About four miles. Going west.'

Breakenridge waited as Hale uncorked his water bottle and trickled some of the contents down his throat.

'One vehicle,' he said finally. 'Couldn't make out what it was.' He replaced the water bottle on his hip.

'Warn Tillman,' Breakenridge said thoughtfully. 'Then get back out there and keep watching.'

He stood watching Hale wheel away, then turned and waited for the rearguard. As it came up, he fell in beside Willard.

'They're going to be waiting for us at the airstrip, I guess.'

Willard grimaced tiredly. 'So they finally worked it out.'

'Was always just a matter of time, Sam.'

'We fight?'

'No choice.'

'You're putting a lot of faith in that crazy Australian.'

'Without the radio that's all we got goin' for us!'

'Yeah. The radio. And the girl. Whoever it was is right there.'

He stared grimly at the line of figures up ahead.

Breakenridge eased forward the last few feet to join Willard just below the top of the slight rise.

'What have we got, Sam?'

'Quarter of a mile in front. The airstrip. They're waiting for us, all right.' Willard passed him the binoculars. 'Take a look. Two o'clock. Old quonset hut. At least two men. Ten o'clock. Three men dug in near the windsock. Another behind some oil drums.'

Breakenridge shielded the binocular lenses with cupped hands to guard against reflections from the early afternoon sun, then slowly raised his head.

The quonset leapt into his vision. Sand had piled up around its base. In places it was almost level with the windows, which were still, surprisingly, intact. The hut itself, although obviously old, seemed to have been kept in good repair. If there were men in there, they were lying low.

He switched to the windsock and counted three men dug in, close to the base of the pole. His gaze moved to the oil drums directly in front of him. The tip of a rifle showed above one of them. About to slide back behind the cover of the rise, he suddenly checked and raised the binoculars slightly, studying the landing strip itself.

It was made up of sectioned steel mesh, a familiar enough sight to him from the past. But something was missing. Something important. What the hell was it? He lowered the glasses, knuckling the raw tiredness from his eyes, trying to think. He put the glasses back to his eyes, searching for the answer. The mesh glittered, myriad reflections bouncing off it in the direct rays of the sun. Then he knew!

Hurriedly he switched to the limp windsock, then across to the hut, altering focus to bring it into close-up. Poking out from the rear end of the hut was part of the front fender and wheel of a jeep. Almost as he registered it, a man in uniform stepped abruptly into his line of vision, lifting field glasses to look directly at their position.

Breakenridge dropped back beside Willard. Sam took one look at his face and knew something was drastically wrong.

'What is it?'

Breakenridge gave him a bleak stare. 'I told you, no loose ends, Sam.'

Willard looked at him in bewilderment. 'What the hell are you talking about?'

'Remember the officer we kept bumping into? The one at the fort?'

'Sure I do. He's dead.'

'Well you better start believing in resurrection. 'Cos he's standing out there right now waiting to blow our fuckin' heads off.'

Willard started to move. Breakenridge grabbed his arm, pulling him back.

'Don't bother. He's got field glasses trained right at us.' The savagery in his voice hacked into Willard like a cleaver.

Breakenridge got to his feet. 'You used up your one mistake.' It was a warning.

The others sprawled, almost prostrate with heat exhaustion, watching listlessly as the two men approached. Breakenridge harried them to their feet remorselessly, cuffing them into life, snarling into blank, dazed faces. He needed one more effort from them, and by Christ he intended getting it.

'Sam! Take Lachasse an' Tillman. Circle around to the left. You got the three by the windsock. Bauer! Take centre. There's a man behind some oil drums at six o'clock. He's yours.'

The German nodded his bandaged head and trudged off up the slope.

'Now! You civilians! I want all of you up on that rise. To the right of Bauer. You'll see a hut. When I give you the word, you open up. Single shots. Keep firing. Make sure you hit the target. Move out an' keep your heads down.'

He shoved them into movement, aware of their fear now that the moment to hit back had come. The only one among them who showed any outward confidence was Matis. Their eyes met and locked briefly.

'What do I do?' Hale slouched on his bike, wiping a rag over his Smith & Wesson.

'Stay where you're at 'till I call for you.'

'And me,' Guillard said huskily. 'Surely you have something in mind.'

Breakenridge swung round. 'You,' he said viciously, 'are a double-crossing, lyin' son-of-a-bitch. An' I'd sure as hell like to cut your throat.'

Guillard stepped back a pace. The blade of a knife glittered suddenly in his hand, arm rigid, the point aimed at Breakenridge's belly.

'Here's the knife. Why don't you try, American?'

Breakenridge stood motionless. 'Mebbe I will. But before I do, I want to know why you didn't tell me that airstrip was functional. It's been in use for a long time. Must have shown up on photographs. The ones you didn't let me see!'

Guillard shrugged slightly, not taking his eyes off the big man for a moment. 'If you remember, coming to this place was not my idea. We should have gone back up the road as I had planned. In twenty-four hours we would have been across the border. But you never had any intention of doing it my way. Always, for you, it was the airstrip.'

'Like I told you right at the start, Guillard, your way would never have worked.'

'Has yours?' Guillard's voice mocked the big man.

Breakenridge remained icy calm. 'We're alive. Tuck'll be here any time now.'

'That pig,' Guillard sneered.

'An' before he touches down, that strip's gotta be cleared. So why don't you jes' shove that oversized toothpick back where you got it from an' go give Bauer a hand.'

He turned his back on the Frenchman and strode off up the slope towards the civilians. Guillard stood glaring after him, feeling angry and slightly foolish. Once again the man had put him at a disadvantage, had made him feel small. The score was adding up. Slowly he returned the knife to the sheath on his hip.

'Glad you didn't try and use that thing, mate.'

Startled, Guillard turned. Hale was grinning at him, the Magnum held negligently in his hand.

Breakenridge crouched down beside the civilians, a few feet below the skyline.

'When you hear firing from the left, move up and blast the hut. That's all you gotta do. Ignore anything else goin' on around you. If you let up on 'em, they'll fire back. So jes' make sure you keep the bastards pinned down.' He scanned their faces. 'Understand?'

There were nods. His eyes met Stephane's. 'We'll do our best, m'sieur,' de Payeux said quietly.

Breakenridge thumbed over the safety selector on the AR-15, settled the weapon in his hands and balanced himself, ready to move.

'Stand by,' he whispered.

There was a ripple of movement as each one prepared to follow his lead. When the action started, he knew they'd be all right. Waiting was the worst time of all, especially for amateurs.

The seconds ticked by. Still nothing from Willard and the others. But he had to wait. Premature action on his part could catch Sam out in the open. Come on, he urged silently. Move it, fercrissake!

A faint indefinable sound broke the stillness. He cocked his head, listening, straining to analyse it. He saw the others lift their heads, looking at him. The sound grew louder, a steady droning coming from the north. Then he recognised it.

A plane!

He slithered down the incline and came to his feet, searching the sky to the north. At first he could see nothing, just a brazen cloudless bowl. His eyes narrowed to slits as he tried to locate it. Then it was there. A dot, coming in low about a mile away, the sound of its engines now plainly to be heard. It grew in size and shape, head-on to him, the shimmering waves of ground heat distorting its outline and making it difficult to identify.

He blinked the sweat out of his eyes, concentrating, willing it not to be an Algerian troop carrier. Then all at once he recognised its silhouette: the old faithful work-horse of the sky. A Dakota. He felt a thrill of exhilaration run through him. It had to be Tuck!

The DC-3 seemed to hover maddeningly just out of reach, like a huge dragonfly. Then, suddenly it was there, roaring along, fifty feet above the ground parallel to the airstrip on the far side of it. Plainly visible in the open fuselage doorway was a man. As it reached the end of the strip, the pilot opened the throttles and the machine banked into a climbing turn to the left.

Breakenridge watched as it came towards him, low and straight. He raised his arms.

'You beautiful fat sweaty Australian bastard,' he yelled.

His words were drowned in the bellowing of the twin Pratt & Whitneys as the aircraft flashed over him, the prop-wash buffeting his body and raising a miniature sandstorm in its wake. He found himself running back up the slope, shoving and pushing at the others.

'Open fire,' he yelled.

At that precise moment a rattle of gunfire came from his left.

It was Willard, opening up on the soldiers dug in by the windsock. Then everyone was firing. In the fraction of a second before he went into action he saw Stephane and Jean-Paul alongside each other, AR-15s snugged in against their shoulders, squeezing off round after round into the hut.

He fired a full magazine at the edge of the hut, trying to punch the rounds through it to immobilise the jeep on the other side. Slapping a fresh mag home with the heel of his hand, he slid back and ran crouching towards Bauer and Guillard.

A burst of fire from the airstrip sowed a line of bullets along the slope above their hastily lowered heads. Breakenridge flung himself down beside them.

'We can't get at him.' The filthy bandage around Bauer's face showed fresh blood where the stock of the AR-15 had pounded against it during firing.

Breakenridge glanced back down to where Hale sat astride the Yamaha.

'Keep trying,' he snapped.

He became aware of the deep-throated hammering of the Dakota's engines. He looked up. Once again it was coming in low and fast from the north. What the hell was Tuck doing? There was no way he could land while the Algerians held the airstrip.

He rolled down the slope, came to his feet and ran to Hale. Suddenly the world was full of thundering aero engines and the rattle of gunfire. Looking back, he saw the man in the open doorway of the aircraft spraying the airstrip with a sub-machine gun.

Flinging himself astride the pillion, he shouted at Hale: 'Take a wide sweep out to the right. Try an' come in on the far side of that hut. Go!'

Hale rammed the machine into gear, opened the throttle and they were away, leaping over the undulating ground, Breakenridge hanging on grimly.

After the Dakota made its pass, it came back again, this time from the south, undercarriage and flaps down. As the Yamaha broke out into the open, heading for the hut, Breakenridge saw the plane touch down at the far end of the strip, bounce once, then settle and run on.

Suddenly, a figure dived through the shattered rear window of the quonset to land beside the jeep. Hale swung the Yamaha right-handed to allow Breakenridge the angle to cut the man down. Before he could do so, the man raised a hand gun, steadied it and fired.

The Yamaha jerked violently sideways as though hit by a giant fist, wrenching the handlebars from Hale's grasp. Ground and sky spun madly in front of Breakenridge's eyes.

He slammed into the hard-packed sand with bone-jarring force. He lay stunned, trying to collect reeling senses. As if from a great distance he heard an engine start and the clash of gears, the sound sharp over that of the taxiing aircraft. The jeep!

His spinning mind forced his body into movement. Somehow he was on hands and knees, vision slowly steadying. The jeep was past him, picking up speed, heading for the Dakota, and he knew there was nothing he could do to stop it.

Then unbelievably he saw someone running. It was Hale. The Englishman hurled himself onto the fast-moving vehicle, arm snaking out to lock round the driver's neck, wrenching him away from the wheel. Out of control, the jeep careered off at an angle. The off-side front wheel struck the Yamaha, and with a resounding crash of buckling metal the jeep flipped over onto its back.

Breakenridge found himself on his feet, stumbling towards the wreck. Reaching it, he looked down. Hale was dead, his body pinned beneath the ruined vehicle, blood trickling from nose and mouth. One arm was outflung as if trying to reach the final few yards to the Dakota. Beside him, neck at an impossible angle, face contorted in a final mask of hatred, was the captain.

He heard voices, people shouting hoarsely, the sound of running feet. The Dakota had completed its turn at the end of the strip, waiting, propellers whirling in glittering arcs. Someone was waving urgently from the open doorway. His arm was grabbed.

'Come on! Move! Let's get the hell out of this!'

It was Sam. Breakenridge saw Tillman, Bauer, Guillard, Lachasse hurrying the civilians towards the plane. Sam was shouting at him again, the words making no impression. There was something he had to do before he left this place, something important.

He pushed Sam away, bent down and picked up a map case from beside the jeep, ripping out the sheets and balling them in his hand. He saw Sam staring at him blankly.

'Get on the plane,' he said thickly. 'I'll be right with you.'

As Willard backed away from him, he took the silver Dunhill from his pocket, snapped it into flame and touched it to the crumpled paper which flared instantly. He stepped back, then tossed the burning mass towards the gasoline leaking from the engine. As he turned away there was a heavy 'thwump' from the fuel as it ignited in a searing flash of heat.

He started towards the plane, then stopped. The lighter was still in his hand. He looked down at it for a moment, turned and flung it at the blazing jeep. Then he ran.

CHAPTER EIGHTEEN

Tuck's meaty hands held the yoke back firmly, the Pratt & Whitneys straining at full power, clawing for air as the Dakota gained height. Behind and below, the airstrip dwindled, a thin black column of smoke lifting skywards at its far end. He took his right hand off the controls and jabbed a finger towards the window on his left. Breakenridge leaned forward over his shoulder, staring out and down. A line of fast-moving vehicles was moving in from the south.

Tuck brought the aircraft round in a smooth bank to the right, levelled off on a westerly heading and passed the controls over to his co-pilot, a skinny young man with an innocent-looking freckled face.

'Now don't go fuckin' wild, sport,' he admonished the other. 'Remember this is a historical aircraft. Gonna present it to the nation one day.'

The young man grinned then concentrated on flying.

Tuck half turned in his seat and looked at Breakenridge. 'Good labour is hard to find these days. I have to make do with raw prawns like the bleedin' Red Baron over there. How are you, sport? Been enjoyin' the good life?'

Breakenridge laughed and shook his head. Right now he wouldn't have swopped the fat Australian for a shipload of champagne and a life ticket to the Rams.

'How the hell did you know we were there? Our radio got busted.'

Tuck shrugged. 'Came over yesterday for a look. No sign of you, so I popped over again today. Just as well, 'cos where would you have been without Uncle Don an' his merry man?'

'A day late an' a dollar short.'

'That croissant cruncher still with you? I want a word in his fuckin' ear about that airstrip. Could have been like Bondi on the Jewish New Year.'

'He's still with us,' Breakenridge said shortly.

Tuck saw the look on his face and decided not to pursue it. 'So what exciting things have you been up to?'

Breakenridge stared ahead through the windshield, remembering.

'It's a long story, Don. I'll tell you some day.'

'If it's got no sex in it, don't bother, mate.' Tuck reached down beside his seat and came up holding a hip flask. 'Got some lemonade for you.'

Breakenridge unscrewed the top and took a drink. The whisky burned into his raw throat.

Tuck jerked a thumb over his shoulder. 'You told the pilgrims about the pay-off yet?'

'Uhuh.' Breakenridge shook his head. 'Figured on saving the best bit till the end.'

Tuck grinned. 'Let me know when you do. I just gotta see their faces, sport.'

He took over the controls again. The Dakota droned steadily on through the afternoon, keeping as low as possible to avoid radar contact.

Breakenridge strapped himself into the radio operator's seat behind Tuck, closed his eyes and tried to relax. They were far from being out of it yet, and worry nagged at the edge of his mind. The sun, beating down on the cockpit, turned it into a sauna bath. Ahead the ground began to rise in the broken jumble of the Djebel Quarkziz. Somewhere beyond, unseen at this ground-hugging altitude, lay the Anti-Atlas mountains and Morocco.

The Australian nursed the aged plane upwards through nine thousand feet, hugging the contours of the hills as they rose beneath them. Occasionally a thermal of superheated air caught the DC-3, flinging it about the sky. Tuck cursed vividly as he wrestled to bring the aircraft back on an even keel.

Breakenridge decided it was time he went back and checked on the others. Also, there was something he had to tell Tillman. He reached down to unbuckle the safety strap about his middle. Abruptly, the Dakota tried to stand on one wing as Tuck flung it violently to the right. In the same instant a black shadow flashed over the cockpit, followed a split second later by the ear-splitting crack of a jet engine.

'Jesus H. Christ!' Tuck yelled as he fought the Dakota back into level flight. 'What the fuck was that?'

'Fighter!'

The young co-pilot was staring out of his side window.

'Where?'

'Way off to starboard. Hang on, he's turning. Coming back!'

They could see it now, banking onto a parallel course. The high tailplane and sharply swept-back wings identified it as a MiG-19. Algerian Air Force insignia stood out boldly in the westering sun. As it flashed past less than two hundred feet away, they saw the wings wagging from side to side. It was the international signal to put down.

Tuck glanced at the helmeted head visible in the other cockpit. 'Bet he does that to all the girls,' he said, almost conversationally. 'Oi, Richthofen!'

The co-pilot glanced at him. Tuck pointed to the flap and undercarriage controls.

'When I tell you, operate them like greased lightning. Make believe you're in a fuckin' Fokker!'

The MiG banked across in front of the Dakota in a tight turn to port.

'Stand by.'

Tuck watched the fighter gain altitude, then side-slip and dive straight for him.

'Hold it . . . hold it. NOW! Flaps and undercart!'

It felt as though the Dakota had run into a concrete wall. Shuddering and groaning, it staggered through the air like a punch-drunk boxer, engines shaking in their mountings as Tuck pulled back on the throttles.

Breakenridge just had time to see flashes of cannon fire split the air in front of them. Then the fighter screamed overhead, shaking them with the thunder of its passing.

'Flaps and gear up,' Tuck shouted as he slammed the throttles open and pushed the nose down. The Dakota dropped like a lift that has snapped its cable. The ground came rushing up at them. At the last moment, Tuck hauled on the control column, bringing the nose up.

'Wish that fuckin' film director was here now,' Tuck yelled.

On either side of them, jagged hills lifted from the tortured earth, threatening them with instant destruction. Tuck weaved the Dakota through them on a switch-back course.

'Where's that bastard now?'

The co-pilot craned his neck, searching the sky.

'Come on,' Tuck urged him, 'this is getting bloody dangerous.'

'I can see him. Right over us. About two thousand.'

'What's he doing?'

'Scratching his head.'

'Watch it,' Tuck snarled. 'I do the funnies around here.'

'What d'you think I am,' shouted the co-pilot, 'a bloody mind-reader?'

Breakenridge sat listening to this interchange with disbelief.

'Don't be bloody disrespectful to your captain,' shouted Tuck. 'I'll have you polishing the wheel nuts when we get back.'

He concentrated on his flying for a few minutes.

After a while the co-pilot said: 'Can't see him.'

'I don't wonder at it with your eyesight,' Tuck said insultingly.

The co-pilot ignored it and winked over his shoulder at Breakenridge.

'I saw that,' said Tuck.

They flew on. Suddenly they were over a high ridge, the ground falling away below. Tuck pointed through the windshield. Ahead, the gleaming flanks of mountains reared up in their path.

'Morocco, mates. Land of the humid and hairy. Which is why that fighter jockey took off!'

He banked the Dakota gently to the left and away from the mountains. Somewhere in front of them lay the Atlantic.

Breakenridge stood in the centre of the aircraft, surveying the people who had come so far with him, balancing himself easily on the balls of his feet as the aircraft floor rose and fell under him. He caught Sam's eye and nodded briefly. This was the moment.

'Under each of your seats you'll find a lifejacket and parachute. We're gonna use 'em.'

He waited, seeing shocked disbelief and fear register on the faces of the ex-hostages, then held up a hand, forestalling the expected protests and questions.

'Hold it.' His voice rose commandingly. 'Don't get worked up. It ain't as bad as it sounds. It'll be what's called a static-line drop. If you look up, you c'n see a cable running fore and aft. Got it?'

Heads lifted unwillingly.

Breakenridge saw the fury on Guillard's face and ignored it. 'My men will now fit the 'chutes on you. On each one you'll see a long canvas strop with a steel hook on the end. One of us will clamp it on the cable. Then all you have to do is walk to the door and step out. The rest is all done for you.'

'Why cannot we land?' Matis struggled half out of his seat.

'Because,' Breakenridge drawled, 'this ain't a seaplane. As simple as that.'

They stared at him, none of them wanting to believe what they'd just heard. Suddenly, Guillard was on his feet, facing him.

'You're mad,' he shouted. 'Playing stupid games. You'll kill us all. I refuse utterly to co-operate. All of you stay where you are. I order it as a representative of the French Government.'

'You all done? Breakenridge asked.

Guillard opened his mouth to reply. Breakenridge took two paces forward and swung a vicious right cross to the Frenchman's jaw. As he collapsed, Breakenridge said: 'Any more questions?'

Nobody spoke.

He nodded to Willard. 'Get on with it, Sam.'

Stephane sat watching as Lachasse and Willard began hauling out parachute packs and lifejackets from under the seats. Sick fear clawed at her stomach as she thought about what lay ahead of her. She felt a hand on her shoulder and looked up. Breakenridge's slate-grey eyes stared down into hers. The normally hard lines of his face had softened a fraction.

'Don't worry,' he said quietly. 'Trust me.'

She covered his hand with her own, holding it tightly as if to draw strength from him. Unable to speak, she nodded, her eyes wide with fear. She felt his hand turn and squeeze hers, gently.

'Wouldn't let anything happen to you. I promised to buy you a drink sometime, remember?'

He disengaged his hand from hers and moved forward. She saw him stop by Tillman and say something to him. The two men moved to the cockpit door and stopped.

Breakenridge spoke in short clipped sentences, underlining some words with sharp jabbing hand-movements. Once Tillman turned to look along the body of the aircraft. Breakenridge held his arm in a vice-like grip. The big Negro turned back, listening as Breakenridge spoke urgently. Stephane saw Breakenridge drop his hand. The two men stood face to face like two huge cats, one seeking domination over the other. Finally Tillman turned and came back down the aircraft, past her seat.

Breakenridge went onto the flight deck and stood behind Tuck. Ahead through the windshield burned the red ball of the lowering sun. Two thousand feet below them the Atlantic shimmered, a dull pewter wasteland.

'There it is, sport. Right on the nose.'

Tuck pointed off to his right. A large grey-painted fishing vessel was hove-to, a couple of miles away. He brought the plane round in a wide circle and flew towards it.

As they passed overhead, Breakenridge looked down. The vessel was one of the big deep-sea boats from the Canary Islands. Alongside were three speedboats. He saw men running along her open foredeck. A lamp blinked out from the bridge. Then they were past.

'You told 'em?' Tuck queried.

Breakenridge nodded.

'Everything?'

'Not quite. I'm saving the surprise right to the last.'

'You foxy old bastard,' said Tuck. 'And you conned him into it.'

When Breakenridge came off the flight deck with the co-pilot, they were all ready. Not willing. Just ready. Yellow lifejackets showed under tight parachute harnessing. He felt the plane bank as it turned for its final run.

Moving clumsily, Sam helped him into his gear. The Dakota was now descending to the dropping altitude.

'Hook up!'

The cry was taken up by Bauer and Lachasse. Quickly, strops were hooked over the cable. Breakenridge made a hurried check of the jumping order. Jean-Paul would be first out, followed by de Payeux, Stephane, Guillard, Talmont and Matis. The first of his own men would be Tillman.

The co-pilot unlocked the door, heaved it inboard, pivoted it against the fuselage and locked it off. Immediately the door was opened, the engine sound rose to a cacophonous roar, blasting painfully at eardrums. The hurricane-force wind raised dust and sand from every nook and cranny. The interior of the aircraft rapidly grew to resemble a jack-hammer factory on piecework.

The co-pilot plugged in his headset. They waited as the plane dropped lower and lower, clutching at ribs and bulkhead spars for support. The young Australian raised his right arm and screamed over the din at them: 'Stand by!'

The whole line shuffled forward and Jean-Paul stood in the open doorway, hands braced against its sides. Staring down, he could see the sea racing by below him. Then the fishing boat came into view, and the three tiny speedboats moving outwards from it. Breakenridge stepped in close behind him to act as jump master.

'Go!'

Jean-Paul was gone. In rapid succession the others stepped out into the void, static-lines jerking out the canopies above them. The speedboats circled like waiting sharks below.

As Matis stepped to the doorway, Breakenridge grabbed his shoulder and turned him round to face inwards. Tillman moved in fast to stand in front of him. He grabbed him by his harness and pulled Matis' face close.

'Marie-Claire,' he screamed into the startled man's face. He saw Matis' head jerk back as if he'd been struck. The big Negro's large hand reached up and unhooked the other's static-line.

'No!'

'Think about her on the way down.' Tillman stiff-armed him backwards through the open doorway and out into space, to plummet to his death in the waiting grave of the sea.

Guillard lay gasping on the floorboards of the speedboat as

a grinning Spanish fisherman hauled Stephane on board. The tiny craft rocked crazily as she flopped down beside him. He sat up groggily, gulping air into his lungs, and stared across at the other two boats. He saw Talmont and de Payeux in one, waving jauntily at him, and the lone figure of Jean-Paul in the other. Quickly he turned his head, scanning the slow swell of the sea. It was empty. Then he heard the bellow of the Dakota low overhead. He looked up.

Standing in the doorway was Breakenridge. Guillard stared up, waiting for him to jump. Then, suddenly, he knew!

'He's beaten you!'

He heard Stephane's triumphant voice in his ear and turned. There was a mocking smile on her face. 'He always will.'

The Dakota gradually dwindled to a speck in the evening sky. Then it was gone.